CHARMS & CHAPTERS

A LIBRARY WITCH MYSTERY

ELLE ADAMS

"Don't drop the cage!" my cousin Cass warned me, backing out into the main section of the library's third floor. The cage in question floated behind us, propelled by Cass's magic. Her long curly red hair was twisted into a topknot out of her face, while water soaked her silver-edged black cloak.

I opened my Biblio-Witch Inventory—a small black book with a silver insignia on the cover—and tapped the word *fly*. The small black-covered book glowed as my magic combined with Cass's, steadying the cage. Inside it, Cass's pet kelpie growled at me through the bars. *This could go really wrong, really fast.*

The majestic white-and-blue-haired water horse, who Cass had christened Swift, had washed up on the beach a few weeks ago. While he'd come to trust me almost as much as he did Cass, that trust probably didn't extend to letting me levitate him down three flights of stairs in our family's magical library. I walked backwards, glancing at the floor behind me every other step in case it disappeared—which wouldn't be the first time. Until now, I'd never levitated anything bigger than a pencil, but letting Cass attempt to single-handedly release a wild kelpie into the ocean was bound to end in disaster. Just another day in the life of a biblio-witch.

Sylvester, my family's owl familiar, flew over our heads, letting out a hoot of derision. "Are you trying to cause an accident?"

"Her idea, not mine," I said to him.

Sylvester snorted. He was a large tawny owl whose wings spanned the length of my shoulders when extended and was generally friendlier to Cass than he was to me. That he was laughing at both of us wasn't a good sign, but I could hardly back out now.

Cass and I had been at odds since I'd first moved to the library, and she'd shocked me when she'd revealed she'd rescued Swift after she'd found him injured on the beach. After she'd spent my entire first week at the library trying to drive me away because she expected that I'd run off like my dad did, I'd decided the best way to mend things between us was to help her take care of her new friend.

As we manoeuvred the cage between the bookshelves, Swift snorted and shook his head, expressing his displeasure.

"Sorry," I muttered to him. "The tank was too heavy to levitate downstairs and if the water had overflowed, the library would have flooded."

We'd already caused a flood when we'd moved the reluctant kelpie from the tank to the cage, which one of us would have to clean up later if we wanted to avoid Aunt Adelaide's wrath. Cass's mother had long since stopped trying to interfere in her daughter's wild schemes, while Estelle was busy with a tutoring session. Meanwhile, Aunt Candace had laughed hysterically when I'd asked if she'd like to help us and declared that she'd prefer to live long enough to write the whole event into one of her books.

"You're dripping everywhere," Sylvester said from above me.

I gritted my teeth, lifting my cloak off the ground. Like Cass's, it had dragged in the water we'd spilt on the upper floor.

"Talk to me when I'm not trying to keep a cage in the air." I did a kind of sideways shuffle towards the staircase down to the second floor, ignoring the owl's comments. The spell's effectiveness depended on me keeping my attention on the cage, and I'd prefer not to find out how much damage a water horse could do to my family's seemingly endless collection of rare books.

I tested the stairs one step at a time, holding onto the bannister for balance with my free hand in case a step disappeared again. Cass walked along behind the hovering cage, grumbling.

"Hurry up," she said. "The sooner we get down these stairs, the better."

"Wouldn't you rather we get downstairs in one piece?" I hopped off the last step, my soaking wet cloak tangling around my ankles. I caught myself before I lost my balance. "I don't understand why you didn't want to use a transportation spell to get him directly into the sea without any of this nonsense."

"I don't want him to panic," said Cass.

I rolled my eyes. Cass was surprisingly sensitive when it came to dealing with animals. People... not so much.

Keeping one eye on the cage, I crossed the second floor, weaving in and out of the towering stacks. The bookshelves moved out of our way at Cass's command. She had better control over the library than I did, luckily for both of us. The cage dripped a trail of water onto the thick carpet, and I swore under my breath. "Aunt Adelaide will have us cleaning this up all night."

"Relax, the library will deal with it in a second," she said confidently.

I'd take her word for it, but Cass had an irritating habit of vanishing whenever there was any real work to be done. I opened my mouth to say so, and the floor moved underneath my feet, causing my cloak to tangle around my ankles again. I tripped, arms pinwheeling, and crashed to the carpet. As I did so, the cage dipped in mid-air. Cass swore, hitting her Biblio-Witch Inventory with her pen. "Get back on your feet, idiot."

"I didn't move the floor on purpose." I scrambled back to my feet. "Anyway, this kind of magic is way beyond my level."

"Grade One lessons are beyond your level," she said waspishly. "But you're the only person who will help me, and it's too late to put the cage back now."

Swift snorted and tapped a hoof, distressed by the cage's rocking movements. I didn't blame him. "Sorry," I whispered to the cage, tapping the word *fly* in my Biblio-Witch Inventory again.

Sylvester flew over our heads with an amused cackle. "I can't believe you're carrying it all the way to the sea using magic."

I backed up a step, holding my cloak off the ground. "Care to lend a hand, or are you just going to laugh at us from up there?"

Sylvester clucked his beak. "I thought I'd shout words of discouragement as well."

"Some familiar you are."

Not that Sylvester was in any way a typical familiar. As far as I knew, the only magic he had was the ability to talk. He took his job as the library's security guard, assistant and rodent-killer very seriously, but got entirely too much enjoyment out of any disaster that befell me.

Cass and I directed the cage down the second staircase to

the first floor. I wiped sweat from my forehead. Just one staircase to go.

A cough drew my attention to the balcony which overlooked the lobby. Aunt Candace stood there with her notebook and pen, wearing an expectant look on her face. Knowing her, she hoped the kelpie would make a bolt for it, so she'd be able to record the event for use in a future novel. Not many people knew Aunt Candace was a bestselling author apart from our family, and she guarded her pen names fiercely. Like the rest of us, Aunt Candace had curly red hair and a pale face dusted with freckles. She was tall and willowy and wore her hair loose, wild tangles flowing to her waist. She grinned and waved at us as we floated the cage past her.

"I can't wait to see what my sister says when that thing escapes," she said.

"Nice to know you all have so much faith in me." I kept my attention firmly on the cage, determined not to screw up now we were so close to the end.

I'd expected at least one of my aunts to kick up a fuss about us levitating Swift right through the middle of the library, but Aunt Adelaide was as hands-off a supervisor as it was possible to be. It was a welcome change from my previous job as a bookshop assistant, where Abe, my dad's former business partner, had constantly nit-picked on my mistakes. Up until a few short weeks ago, I'd assumed he would be the closest I'd ever have to a family. Then three vampires had shown up at the shop where I worked as Abe's assistant and nearly set the place on fire in an attempt to steal a mysterious journal Dad had left in the shop's back room.

The spell Aunt Adelaide had set up to protect me had also awakened my own magic, which Dad had been forced to hide from me since my mum had been a normal, and the magical rules stated that non-paranormals weren't allowed to know about this world. Despite that rule, the magical laws seemed quite lax at times, though it didn't hurt that my family *made* the rules. In the library, at least. Using hostile magic was strictly forbidden, but as Cass had pointed out a dozen times that week alone, no law prevented her from keeping dangerous pets.

It could be worse. At least it's not a chimera. I'd had a crash-course in all things paranormal over the last three weeks since I'd moved here, and the library threw another surprise at me each day. I reached the final staircase, skipping the missing top step—and the second step vanished, too.

I tripped, grabbing the bannister, and the Biblio-Witch Inventory fell from my hand, tumbling downstairs.

Cass shouted aloud. The cage dipped in mid-air, and I panicked, grabbing it with my hand. There was no way I could support its weight without magic, so I let go and jumped out of the way as the cage crashed onto the stairs. The door burst open, and the kelpie leapt over my head, splattering me with water. Flat on my back, I lifted my head in time to see Swift land at the foot of the stairs and run full-tilt across the ground floor.

Shouts rang out from below as the giant white horse circled the lobby, causing patrons to dive behind bookshelves and stacks of books to topple over.

"You idiot!" screamed Cass, running downstairs. She jumped the last few steps and sprinted between the shelves to the front desk. "You left the cage unlocked!"

"You told me to!" *I knew something like this would happen.* I scrambled to my feet, grabbing my sopping wet cloak in one hand to avoid tripping again, and ran downstairs to retrieve my Biblio-Witch Inventory—entirely too late. There was no chance of recapturing the kelpie now he'd tasted freedom.

I skidded to a halt in the reception area, the carpet

considerably wetter than it'd been earlier. Catching up to Swift on foot was an impossibility—there was a good reason for his name. "Cass, we have to transport him to the sea. He's not domesticated—"

"He doesn't want to hurt anyone, he wants to play," Cass insisted.

I opened my mouth to say she was deluded, but she was right. Swift had picked up a book in his mouth and threw it at a crowd of students, who scattered.

"He wants to play fetch," I told them.

The students didn't look convinced. One of them had fainted. Another threw a book at the kelpie in defence. I ran and caught the leather-bound book before it made contact and put it on the desk.

Swift completed another circuit around the lobby. If I didn't know better, I'd say he was enjoying the attention.

"Over here!" Cass said, jumping up and down in front of the front doors and waving both arms.

"Use the spell," I said, running towards her.

"I don't need to," she said insistently. "He recognises my voice."

Sure enough, Swift turned his long head in our direction. Then he launched into a sprint, so fast his hooves hardly seemed to touch the ground.

"Uh, Cass, I don't think he's going to stop if we don't move."

"Don't be absurd."

The kelpie kept running.

"Cass, seriously."

I grabbed her arm and yanked her to the side, and the kelpie soared past, knocking open the oak doors and leaping into the town square.

Cass gave me a furious look. "You—"

"If I'd tried to stop him, he'd have knocked me out." I

caught the left-hand door before it slammed closed, and the cold sea breeze buffeted me in the face. Around the town square, panicking shoppers fled the escaped kelpie's path.

I hopped down the steps into the square. Behind us, the huge brick form of the library dwarfed every other building. It'd always struck me as like a palace or a castle, with its majestic stained-glass windows drawing the eye from miles off, and I could still hardly believe I got to call it home. Even Cass's hissing, "This is all your fault" into my ear at the sight of Swift wheeling around the town square didn't take that away.

"It's *not* my fault," I said. "Anyway, he's having fun."

The kelpie ran at a crowd of Christmas shoppers wearing pointed wizard's hats, who yelped and hid behind one another as he wheeled into the bakery. I heard Zee swearing and ran after him, but he ducked out a moment later, a muffin in his mouth. I should have guessed he'd go there—he'd become a fan of Zee's muffins after I'd fed him one in an attempt to get him to trust me. Oops.

Zee herself emerged from the shop behind Swift, staring in disbelief. Flour stained her warm brown skin and her curly hair was soaked in water. "He wrecked the whole display," she said accusingly.

"Oh, no." I kept one eye on the kelpie, who devoured the muffin in two quick bites. "If it's any consolation, I think he's a fan of your cooking. I'll pay you back—tell my aunt if I'm not back in half an hour. We need to make sure he reaches the ocean first."

"Mum's going to kill you for that," said Cass.

"He's your kelpie," I reminded her.

Swift darted into the flower shop and emerged with a mouthful of peonies.

"Hey!" yelled the shopkeeper.

"I'll pay you back," I called to him, but Swift was already

running to the next shop, scattering flowers everywhere as he did so.

Cass swore. "Now what, genius? Aren't you going to help me get him back into the cage?"

"I think it's a bit late for the cage," I said. "I told you I wasn't an experienced enough witch to get the cage all the way downstairs."

"Well, you should be by now," she said, with a sniff. "What's my sister doing with your training? Or are you spending all your time watching Netflix instead?"

"We're spending a lot of time on magic lessons, actually." Okay, we studied magic with a reward of watching Netflix, but I'd missed out on about a decade of television and hadn't even owned a TV for the last three. It was nice to have a cousin close to my own age, and Estelle had fast become my closest friend here in Ivory Beach. "Look, Cass, if you want to get him to the sea without him wrecking anything else, you're going to have to use magic on him. He won't mind."

"Fine, but if it goes wrong, it's on you." She held up her Biblio-Witch Inventory and tapped on a word.

The horse skidded to a halt and turned to her. "Hey," she said, waving at him. "Come on, we're going to the sea. This way."

She walked to the giant horse, and I hurried to follow her, giving apologetic looks to the passing townspeople.

"Is that a kelpie?" asked Alice from the pet shop, her eyes wide. "I've never seen one before."

"Ah, he washed up on the shore a while ago," I said. "Cass rescued him and we're getting him back to the sea now."

Her brows rose. "Cass did? Really?"

I guess she didn't know about Cass's secret soft spot for animals, either. Though maybe it wouldn't be a secret after today.

Cass stood beside the clock tower. "It's not working," she

said, beckoning to Swift. "Rory, don't just stand there, do something."

"Hey, Swift," I called. "Don't you smell the sea air? You're almost home."

Actually, I had no idea how the kelpie had ended up here, considering they were native to Scotland and we were on the northern English coast, but Swift turned his head towards me. Encouraged, I gestured over my shoulder at the sparkling line of sea in the distance.

Swift jumped, soaring over our heads. Both of us ducked to avoid being hit in the face by a flying talon, and then Cass sprinted after him.

The few people on the seafront moved aside as the kelpie leapt down to the pebbled beach towards the sea. I stopped to clutch at a stitch in my chest, gasping for breath.

Swift swam into the lapping tide, his white-blue coat blending in with the high waves, and was gone.

Cass jumped down to the pebbled beach, walking out to the ocean. The sea lapped around her ankles, stirring her already soaking wet cloak.

"Cass, come back!" I shouted. Even if she was a great swimmer, there was no chance of her catching up to the kelpie.

I hurried down the pebbled beach, stopping at a suitable distance from the lapping waves. "Cass, give it up. It's far too cold to go into the sea."

She ignored me, determinedly wading into the water. I shook my head, then I spotted someone else in the sea, just beneath the pier. A man with blond hair stood ankle-deep in the shallows. *The Reaper.*

Despite his name, he didn't look grim in the slightest— more like an angel, with tousled fair hair that looked white in contrast to his dark clothing and the curved scythe he carried strapped to his back. What was he doing paddling in the sea? He'd once joked about liking swimming just fine despite having the scythe as a permanent accessory, but I'd assumed he'd meant in a recreational sense. Not fully clothed on a winter's day when the water was like an ice bath.

"Hey, Xavier," I called, walking along the beach to him. "What're you doing out here?"

Then I saw what lay tangled in the shallows at his feet.

It was a body.

X avier lifted the body and waded out of the water onto the pebbled bank. Despite the water, his clothes didn't look wet, and he wasn't shivering either. Must be a Reaper thing. The body he placed on the shore, though, was definitely dead. I recognised the emblem on the front of his cloak as belonging to the uniform for the town's academy of magic.

"Who is he?" I asked.

"Haven't a clue," Xavier said. His aquamarine eyes shone with concern. "But his soul was gone by the time I found his body."

"What, there's an aquatic reaper wandering around?" I said, then instantly felt bad for making light of the subject. I didn't know the kid who'd died, but still.

"No, it can't be," said Xavier. "I'm in charge of reaping souls in the town and the surrounding area, so maybe he died outside the town's boundaries and his body washed up here. I'm guessing he drowned, but I can't be certain. Can you call Edwin? I don't have a phone."

"You don't?" That explained why he hadn't given me his

number. Not that I'd thought much about the subject, but the two of us had worked together to catch a murderer and save my aunt from prison. That warranted more than a 'see you around', right?

"I'm not allowed one, according to my boss," he explained.

I frowned. "That's a weird rule. What if you need to make a phone call? I mean, it's not like the ghosts can answer the phone, I guess, but the living can."

I didn't actually know if he had a family. Xavier and I had only seen one another a handful of times since he'd helped me solve the murder that'd taken place in the library in my first week here, but the scythe strapped to his back was the least of his secrets. The rules for Reapers were a mystery even to most of the magical world.

"If someone in my area dies, I'm drawn there by magic," he explained. "My boss can contact me the same way. Generally, there's no phone signal in the afterworld."

"What, that's a place?" I asked, curious. "Or is that classified information?"

"Reapers only. Sorry." He turned back to the boy's body. He was vaguely recognisable as one of the kids who kept coming into the library after school and during study periods. How had he ended up in the water? It might be a Sunday, but all his fellow students were studying for their end-of-term exams in the warmth, or else getting up to mischief. Cass had had to chase two of them out of the kelpie's room this morning.

Speaking of Cass. I turned around, scanning the beach, and spotted her wading out of the shallows, her face screwed up in annoyance.

"Thanks for the help," she yelled at me.

"You can't seriously think I'd have chased an angry kelpie out into the middle of the ocean, can you?" I shook my head.

"Anyway, someone drowned over here. Did you see anyone in the water?"

"Drowned?" Cass waded over to us, dragging her sopping wet cloak behind her. Pulling out her wand, she dried herself with a single flick. "When?"

"Haven't a clue." I shivered, making a mental note to learn how to dry myself off using magic. "Do you know him?"

"Hey, I recognise that dude," said Cass. "He hangs out in the Reading Corner with the academy students after school. They have all their meetings there. You know, chess club and whatever."

"I thought so," I said. "Have you seen him recently?"

"Yeah, just yesterday."

Then he couldn't have been out to sea for long before he'd washed ashore. But then, what might have happened to his soul? Perhaps there truly was a Reaper who lived out in the ocean. If Xavier didn't know, though, I was clueless.

"I'll fetch Edwin." Cass walked across the pebbled shore. The police station wasn't far from the seafront, so it'd be quicker to walk there rather than calling them on the phone.

Xavier carried the body to a bench overlooking the coastline. On our right, the pier jutted out into the ocean, next to the spot where he'd found the body. Perhaps the kid had fallen into the water, but if he'd drowned, his soul would have been Xavier's to take.

"Weird," muttered Xavier. "Maybe there's another Reaper nosing around our territory. I'll have to speak to my boss."

"He definitely drowned, right?" The kid's clammy hand brushed against mine as Xavier laid him on the bench, and I shuddered. I might have helped a police investigation into two murders in the library during my first week here, but I didn't generally make a habit of hanging around the dead— the Reaper being an obvious exception.

"I assume he did. Just what was your cousin doing in the sea, anyway?"

"Looking for the kelpie. Our plan to release him into the ocean didn't quite go as planned." Understatement of the century. At least Swift was back where he belonged and not running amok around the town square. "He can't be blamed for the kid's death, though, considering he's been in the library for the last three weeks."

"Best not to bring 'that up," Xavier commented. "There's Edwin. Let's see what he says about this."

Edwin, the elf who led the local police force, looked positively tiny compared to the two trolls who acted as his main security guards. Their large bodies were crammed into the same blue cloaks worn by all the local police, though despite their bone-crushing muscles, they'd been friendly enough to me. Edwin, on the other hand, wore a scowl on his face, suggesting he hadn't forgotten he'd arrested Aunt Candace on suspicion of a murder she hadn't committed and then had to deal with her endless complaints about not being able to access her manuscript in jail. He'd been almost as glad as the rest of us when she'd turned out to be innocent.

"Where'd you find him?" Edwin asked Xavier.

"He was in the shallows over there, near the pier," explained the Reaper. "His soul's gone, so I assume he died outside my area."

"Or someone cursed his soul into a book again," said Cass, her eyes narrowing at me.

Oh, no. I should have guessed she'd pin the kelpie's departure squarely on me. In fairness, she'd never quite got past the fact that I'd accidentally got Aunt Candace arrested during my first week, when I'd mistakenly accused her of helping the vampire I'd suspected of murdering two people and the police happened to be listening in.

That alone was reason enough to stay out of *this* incident, but I couldn't help feeling guilty when I looked at Xavier. Banishing souls was his job, and the notorious Grim Reaper wasn't known for being a pleasant supervisor.

"There's nowhere his soul could have gone except the afterlife," Xavier said. "But that can't happen without the aid of a Reaper."

"Then discuss the matter with your supervisor," said Edwin. "I, however, will be taking the body with me. Aurora, what are you doing here? Was it you who found the body?"

"I saw Xavier standing in the sea and went to see what he was doing," I explained. "I was helping Cass, er, with her kelpie. Pretty much everyone in the town square saw us on the way. I didn't know there was a body down here until I got up close."

Cass gave me a furious look, but I'd had to give the police an alibi. Besides, given the damage Swift had caused to the town square, Edwin would be neck-deep in complaints by the day's end.

"If that's the case, I'd advise you to leave," said Edwin. "And this time, Aurora, I'd advise you to think carefully before making accusations."

With an apologetic look at Xavier, I turned away from the beach and joined Cass in crossing the road.

"You had to tell everyone, didn't you?" she said.

"I didn't want either of us to get accused of murder," I said. "Also, there isn't a person in town who won't know about Swift by now, I guarantee it."

Cass scowled and marched ahead without speaking to me. *Honestly.* Maybe I'd been right to suspect that trying to get into Cass's good books by being nice was as futile as searching for the library's upper corridor, which had been missing for over a decade.

Back at the library, we found Aunt Adelaide waiting expectantly at the front desk, her arms folded across her chest. She was tall and curvy, like Estelle, and her auburn hair bounced to her shoulders. "Cassandra Hawthorn," she said.

Given that I'd never heard her call Cass by her full name before, I took a wild guess that she and I had crossed a line. My legs locked to the spot, while my heart beat against my ribcage. *I knew I should have talked her out of it.*

"Yes." Cass made to move around the desk but stopped dead at a gesture from Aunt Adelaide.

"Did you hear *any* of my warnings about using your biblio-witch magic on a living creature?" she asked. "And I specifically told you not to drag Rory into your schemes."

"She's the one who didn't lock the cage properly!" Cass protested.

"She was following your directions, which is more than you deserved," said Aunt Adelaide. "You took advantage. I'm ashamed of you."

Shame heated my own cheeks. I should have known helping Cass would come back to bite me. My best friend Laney had said frequently that I needed to be more assertive, but I'd thought taking up my place in the magical world was a sign that I'd moved on from my old habits. Perhaps not.

"Is that all?" Cass said.

"No," said Aunt Adelaide. "From now on, you're to consult me before bringing any animals into the library. *Any* animals. That clear?"

Cass opened her mouth, then closed it, seeing something in her mother's expression that wasn't worth arguing with. "Yeah, whatever."

"I take it you at least managed to get the creature to the sea?" asked Aunt Adelaide.

"Yes," I put in. "The kelpie made a run for it the instant he got free. He couldn't resist chasing a few people, but all he wanted to do was get back in the water."

"Well, of course he did," said Aunt Adelaide. "I take it the entire town witnessed your shenanigans?"

"More or less," I said. "Hey, look on the bright side, Cass. Now they know you have a heart."

Cass looked like she wanted to shrivel me on the spot. "They also know you're an incompetent—"

"Cass!" said Aunt Adelaide. "I doubt your Aunt Candace or myself could have captured a rampaging kelpie without resorting to spells which would have made the situation worse. I assume you've learned your lesson about helping dangerous aquatic monsters. Did Edwin see you?"

"Yes, but only because Xavier found a dead body in the sea," I said. "One of the students who used to come here. Cass said she'd seen him in the library before…"

"I don't know him," she said. "I just recognise him from those kids who come in here after school. I wouldn't know his name."

"Someone drowned?" Aunt Adelaide glanced over her shoulder at the Reading Corner. "I've been too busy restoring things to order to talk to the students here. I suppose we should let their teachers tell them the news."

"Yeah," I said. "The weird thing is his soul was gone, according to Xavier. Like…"

She raised an eyebrow. "Like Duncan?"

"Not sealed in an object," I said. "He said it was like a Reaper already sent the kid's soul to the afterlife, which suggests he died outside Xavier's area. Wherever that is."

"I can't say I'm an expert," she said. "How sad. A student… this isn't the weather to go near the sea, no matter the circumstances."

"It looked like he fell off the pier and drowned, but that *is* Xavier's area." I dug a hand in my pocket, finding it soaking wet from Swift's adventurous escape. My entire cloak was, in fact. I pulled out my bedraggled notebook and pen and put them on the front desk to dry.

"Maybe—" Aunt Adelaide broke off. "Come on out, Candace. There's no need to lurk."

Aunt Candace sidled out from behind a shelf, her pen and notebook floating beside her. Not a surprise. If anyone said the word 'murder', she'd appear with her pen eager and ready, while any dramatic situation—or any word we spoke —was liable to end up on the page.

"Go on," she said, with an expectant look on her face.

Aunt Adelaide shook her head. "I'll leave the speculating to the police. We're not getting involved in this one. I think poor Edwin would be happy to avoid the library for the foreseeable future, besides."

"I wasn't *that* bad," Aunt Candace said. "If anything, the prison needed livening up."

Cass made a disparaging noise. "I'm off. *Not* to do anything with rare animals, before you start on me again, Mum."

Aunt Adelaide tutted, but didn't stop her from sauntering away. "Are you okay, Rory?"

"Sure." I put down my Biblio-Witch Inventory, too, relieved to find the water hadn't caused any damage. "I mean, the dead body kind of freaked me out, but it's pretty normal for Xavier. His boss will probably order him to find out what happened to the victim's soul, like last time."

"Yes, I can't say I've had the pleasure of associating with the leading Reaper," said Aunt Adelaide. "By all accounts, he's very unpleasant. Be careful, Rory."

Aunt Candace looked towards me, an odd smirk on her face. "You worry too much, Adelaide. Rory's capable of making her own decisions. Haven't all of us tried a dalliance with the living dead at one time or other?"

A flush rose to my cheeks. "Xavier and I aren't dating."

19

ELLE ADAMS

Sure, he was kind, and had done his best to make me feel welcome, but he was dedicated to his job. If he wasn't even allowed to own a mobile phone, I doubted the Grim Reaper would look past him dating a human.

Aunt Candace made a sceptical noise in her throat and retreated behind the bookshelves again. "We'll see."

My familiar, Jet, flew to land on my shoulder. He was a little black crow who'd taken a shine to me on my first day here, and despite my initial apprehension, he was a good companion to have when exploring the library's most hazardous corners.

"Hey," I said to him. "How was your day?"

The crow chirped in answer, fluttering onto my shoulder.

"C'mon, let's clear up some of these books."

While Aunt Adelaide had removed the water spillages, the smell of salt water and damp carpets lingered, and several of the books made hissing noises at me when I picked them up. *Gotta love a sentient library.* Luckily, most of them hadn't fallen far from their shelves, so it was a simple matter to pick them up and put them back into place. After the excitement of the day, I welcomed the routine activity.

Over the last few weeks, I'd really begun to carve out my place here in the library. Okay, sometimes the floors vanished, the shelves moved, and doors transformed into walls right when I was about to walk through them, but the library's unexpected magic was as much of an occupational hazard as Aunt Candace turning my misfortune into narratives. Blame my grandmother, who'd died without leaving a clear map of the library, leaving the place riddled with wrong turns, trick staircases and sections that defied the laws of physics. An entire floor was missing at the top and nobody knew how to get to it, there was a vampire sleeping in the basement who'd been there since before I was born, and sometimes the books displayed an alarming level of awareness.

"Ow!" A thorny vine came out of the book that I'd just picked up and hit me in the face. I dropped the book, but the vine extended, wrapping around my arm. Wincing, I dug my free hand in my pocket and remembered too late that I'd left my notebook on the front desk to dry off. *Amateur mistake there, Rory.*

"Hang on," said Aunt Adelaide from behind me, tapping a word in her Biblio-Witch Inventory. The vine withdrew from my arm and snaked back into its book, revealing a plain blank cover with no title on it. I turned it over, finding no number on the spine either. "Sorry. That one has a few defence mechanisms on it. Oh, who is that?"

The door opened at the front of the library and someone walked in. Aunt Adelaide moved to the front desk and put the book down behind the counter, while Edwin and his two troll guards entered the library.

"Edwin," said Aunt Adelaide. "Nice to see you."

"I wish I could say the same," said the elf. "I assume your nieces told you about the student who died on the beach today?"

"Yes, Cass and Rory told me. Are you here to talk to the students?"

"If you don't mind."

From Aunt Adelaide's annoyed expression, she did mind, but she indicated for him to go ahead to the Reading Corner. "Remember we have a number of classes taking place in here who'd appreciate not being disturbed."

"They don't look like they're doing much studying," he remarked. "Looks like they're having a fight."

"Oh, for—" Aunt Adelaide hurried towards the study area, while I approached the elf policeman.

"Do you think it was a murder?" I asked. "Or did he drown by accident?"

"It's inconclusive, but we'd like to know if anyone saw him today before his death," the elf said. "By all signs, he drowned. The positioning of the body suggests he fell from the pier, but we've yet to find any witnesses."

He and the two trolls approached the Reading Corner—the supposed quiet area of the library—where a red-haired girl and a pale kid with glossy black hair sat apart from the others. Judging by their torn cloaks and red faces, they'd been the source of the fight. The two of them glowered at one another and at the teacher who held their wands in his grasp.

Aunt Adelaide tutted as Edwin walked past. "I hoped *not* to involve the library in this murder case," she said in a low voice.

"Maybe he thinks one of the students did it," I said, dropping my voice, too. "In which case, they'll probably do the questioning elsewhere."

The front door opened again, and Xavier entered soundlessly. It was impossible not to stare at the way he moved, unlike anyone else even in the magical world—fast, fluid and otherworldly.

"Oh, hi, Rory," he said. "I'm here to…"

"Question the students?" I guessed. "Did Edwin find out who the victim is, then?"

"The victim's called Andrew Lynch—he already informed the boy's family," said Xavier. "I don't know him. I rarely have reason to pay a visit to the academy or its students."

Probably for the best, considering his job involved escorting the dead into the afterlife.

"Does he think it was an accident?" I asked.

"Yes, he does," said Xavier. "Accidental drowning. But the

way his soul vanished... murder or not, there's something odd at work."

"Someone stole his soul?" I asked. "Like with the book?"

"If that was the case, the object was nowhere near the scene. I'd have sensed it." He frowned. "Or another Reaper came here, but I'd know if they did. I have the ability to detect other Reapers. That's why my boss finds it so easy to contact me."

That sounded like a more extreme version than my old overzealous boss, Abe, but I decided not to mention it. The Grim Reaper probably wasn't the kind of employer who understood boundaries between 'work' and 'home'. Wait, did the Reaper even have a home? He must live somewhere. "You're the only Reaper for the entire town, then?"

"My boss and I are, yes," he said. "Believe it or not, these situations aren't common."

Hmm. "Seems weird that he was alone out here. It's not exactly the weather for a solo trip to the beach. You'd think the other kids from the academy would have noticed he was missing."

"Yes, that's odd, too," he said. "He's as likely to have died of hypothermia than anything, given the temperature of the water. Not that I'm generally aware of such things..."

"Of course not," I said. "Perks of not belonging to the land of the living."

His bright aquamarine eyes seemed to dim a little at those words. "I guess so."

"Not that it's a bad thing," I said quickly. "You look living to me. I mean, you look great, for a dead guy." *Stop talking, Rory.* I didn't typically get tongue-tied around cute guys, Reapers or otherwise, but Xavier was a mile away from the sort of guys I'd associated with before my induction into the magical world. And now I'd just implied that my idea of flattering him was to say he was more appealing than a corpse. Socially adept, I was not.

"I can't say I'm up against strong competition, considering," he said mildly. "But I'll take that as a compliment."

Silently cursing Aunt Candace for putting the image of us dating into my mind, I looked down at the desk to hide my blush. "Maybe the guy who died checked something out of the library."

Xavier blinked, not fooled by my obvious attempt to change the subject. I'd resolved to stay out of the police investigation, but I might as well check the library's record book now I knew the victim's name.

I picked up the record book where Aunt Adelaide had left it on the front desk and skimmed to the most recent page. Sure enough, Andrew Lynch's name was there. And...

The last book he'd checked out was *A Novice's Guide to Vampirism.*

Vampires? *That can't mean anything good.*

3

I put the record book down. That the victim had been reading up on vampires didn't necessarily mean anything was amiss. Students at the magical academy might have a dozen reasons to check out an introductory guide to vampirism, but that he'd checked the book out and taken it home rather than reading it here in the library suggested more than a passing interest. But the book, according to the record, had never been returned. It was a week overdue, actually.

Of course, it didn't help that I was naturally disinclined to trust anything to do with vampires. Back when I'd thought I was a normal, three vampires had tried to steal Dad's old journal and if not for my biblio-witch magic, they'd have killed me. One of the three had been jailed after attacking the library, but the others were still out there somewhere. Dominic had said they were members of a society of hunters for rare artefacts, but since none of us could actually read the journal, nobody knew what they wanted with it. It was unlikely that the death of an academy student was remotely connected to a journal nobody except my family knew about, but I couldn't quell my instant apprehension.

"Rory?" said Xavier, a quizzical look on his face. "Something wrong?"

"Andrew Lynch checked out a beginner's guide to vampirism," I said. "Three weeks ago. Never returned it. Do you think that's suspicious?"

"Not really," he said. "The academy's syllabus covers all paranormals, not just humans, but I'll mention it to Edwin."

I looked for Edwin and spotted him with a group of students over by the Reading Corner. They all clustered around him, talking over one another.

"Excuse me," I said, trying to get Edwin's attention. Instead, a woman turned to Xavier and me. From the shiny badge on her cloak and official-looking, silver-brimmed hat, I assumed she was the teacher who was supervising the students in the library.

"Reaper," she said, wearing the same wary expression that most people had when they spoke to Xavier. "Did you speak to Andrew's spirit after his death?"

"No, I didn't," he said. "Unfortunately, his soul was already gone."

"What do you mean, *gone?*" said the woman.

"I've yet to find out," said Xavier, "but it suggests his death wasn't an accident."

Murmurs rose among the students as they tuned into the conversation.

"What, you think someone murdered one of my students?" she asked.

"Nobody suggested anything of the sort," said Edwin, with a disgruntled expression on his face. "Reaper, I told you to consult with your supervisor before making accusations. In the meantime, I would like to question everyone who knew the victim."

As the students turned their attention to him again, the teacher moved away from the group, her eyes on Xavier. "What in the goddess's name would one of my students have done to lose his soul?"

"I couldn't say," Xavier replied. "I will consult with my boss, of course."

"Andrew Lynch recently checked out a book on vampirism," I said to her. "Any idea why he might have done that?"

"Certainly not out of academic interest," she said. "I don't recall him ever handing in his homework, let alone pursuing extra research."

"Did Andrew show a particular interest in vampires, though?" Had he wanted to become a vampire? I didn't see the appeal, but teenagers might view the situation differently. "Maybe that's why his soul disappeared. He turned into a vampire."

"No," said Xavier. "I can't say I've ever reaped a vampire's soul, but that's because they rarely die."

"Hannah, go back to speak to Edwin," the teacher said to a girl who'd stopped to listen in. "And can you two keep your thoughts to yourselves? By tomorrow, the entire school will think Andrew died in a vampire transformation gone wrong."

"What if it's true?" Xavier asked. "The missing soul and the odd circumstances of his death suggest more than an accidental drowning."

She let out an impatient sigh. "I appreciate the work you do, Reaper... and who exactly are you? The Reaper's assistant?"

I blinked, startled. "No, I work here in the library. I'm Aurora Hawthorn. I was with Xavier when he found the body. That's how I know he checked out a beginner's guide to vampirism last week and never returned it."

She pursed her lips. "I'll ask his family to return the book."

"Never mind the book," I said quickly. "Just, you know, Xavier will get into trouble if he doesn't find the missing soul."

I felt Xavier's surprised eyes on me. Should I not have said that? Or had I implied that I cared more than necessary about whether he got into trouble?

"Well, I suppose it *is* your area," she said grudgingly. "I'll ask if his friends would mind sharing any relevant information with you. The academy does have a number of vampires as students, but most of them sleep during the day at weekends."

"Wait, there are vampires at the academy?" I blinked in surprise. I'd assumed, like the Reaper, that they existed apart from the rest of us.

"Why wouldn't there be?" asked Miss Nolan. "The academy accepts a diverse range of students."

"I thought vampires didn't age," I said. "Does that mean they're stuck in school forever?"

"No," she said. "We have open places at the academy for vampires unfortunate enough to have been bitten before reaching maturity. They leave at eighteen like everyone else."

Huh. I could think of more interesting things to do with immortality than go back to school. Like solving world hunger—or reading all the books in the library. Maybe that's why I wasn't cut out to be one of the living dead. Either way, I really couldn't fathom why vampires had more of a reputation for being sexy and appealing than Reapers did. I'd pick Xavier over them, any day of the week.

"Okay," I said. "Just wondering."

"Well, please try to speculate somewhere my students aren't listening in," she said.

And with that, she walked back to the Reading Corner.

"Oops," I said to Xavier. "I guess I let my curiosity get the better of me."

"No harm in asking questions," he responded. "I think you might be right, for the record."

"What, that he died after turning into a vampire?" I asked. "How does the whole thing work, anyway?" I knew a little, from Dominic, but it was one part of the paranormal world I had little interest in, except for the sake of my own survival.

"Turning into a vampire requires two things," said Xavier. "Firstly, the person has to get bitten. Then they have to drink a vampire's blood. If they just get bitten, the effects fade after a while. Oh, and if someone is fatally injured and a vampire's blood is used to heal the wound, that causes the same transformation. Vampire blood has healing properties, see."

I turned this over in my mind. "Did they find any bite marks on the body?"

"I'll ask," Xavier said, turning to Edwin. He stood between the two students who'd been fighting, both of whom looked disgruntled. Maybe they'd both known Andrew Lynch. "I've never heard of someone losing their soul in the middle of a vampire transformation, but it's not an area I've studied in-depth. There haven't been any new vampires created in my area during my time as a full Reaper."

"Seriously?" I asked. "Are—are you like a vampire, and you don't age?"

"What would give you that idea?"

I shrugged. "I saw you walk out into the middle of the ocean and it looked like the water didn't even touch you."

"I walk between the land of the living and dead," he said. "That means I don't age as long as I carry the scythe. I also don't need to eat or sleep, theoretically. It also means some physical objects can't touch me unless I let them. Makes it easier to find souls that way."

"So you can't die?" Xavier didn't look like any of the

vampires I'd seen, pasty and wax-like. He looked... human. No, more than human. Nobody I'd met had eyes such a crystal-clear shade of aquamarine.

"Not as long as I carry the scythe," he said, shifting position so I could see it poking out from behind him. "I can also get into places no human would normally be able to get into, if it's required for me to reap a soul. But no Reaper keeps the job forever. When the time comes for me to retire, and I give up the scythe, then I'll be able to die like everyone else."

"Huh." And to keep doing his job, he'd have to hold himself apart from the world at large. It seemed a lonely existence. "So why did you pick the job?"

"It's more of a calling," he said. "Very few are born with the Reaping gift, and I was chosen like my dad was before me."

"Reaper," Edwin said, approaching us. "Did you have a question you wanted to ask me?"

"Did you find any bite marks on the body?" asked Xavier.

"No, but we didn't look closely," said Edwin. "That's up to the town healers, who're at the police station right now talking to my assistant."

"Good," said Xavier. "The only explanation I can think of for his missing soul is that something went wrong when he was in the middle of a vampire transformation. I've never heard of such a thing happening before, but it's worth checking for bite marks all the same."

"Wait," said Edwin, looking noticeably more worried. "If he's a vampire... does that mean he might wake up and start walking around?"

"It's possible," admitted Xavier.

The elf policeman paled. "In that case, I have to go and see the body."

"You might need my help," Xavier said. "And Rory can come with me, right? She won't cause trouble."

"I suppose it's better than her staying here and questioning my suspects," said Edwin. "Please *try* not to make a nuisance of yourself."

"I won't cause trouble," I said, a little insulted that he thought me as much of a potential trouble-maker as my aunt was. "Honestly."

The old me would never have tried butting into an investigation that was frankly none of my business. This death hadn't even taken place in the library, so I didn't have any excuse other than burning curiosity and the desire for Xavier not to end up in trouble because of me. If anything, a large part of me wished he hadn't asked me to come. Vampires had terrified me ever since those three strangers had shown up in Dad's shop and turned my world upside-down. Admittedly, that event had led to the best change of my life, but vampires still haunted my nightmares with silent steps and corpse-like smiles.

I have to face my fears someday. Why not today?

By the time we reached the seafront, though, my hands were visibly shaking.

"You okay, Rory?" Xavier whispered, letting the elf go ahead of us into the police station.

"Having second thoughts," I murmured, too quietly for Edwin to overhear. "If Andrew is going to wake up..."

"I don't think he will," Xavier said. "I just figured Edwin might want to check for bite marks. But if the victim was bitten and didn't die, his soul would still be there. There's no way for it to disappear mid-transformation without being reaped. Don't tell my boss I told you that, by the way."

"Learn something new every day." I drew in a deep breath, facing the police station. "I'm ready."

I wasn't, and I think Xavier knew it, but if I wanted to fit into the paranormal world, I needed to get over my fear of vampires.

Edwin ordered me to wait in the lobby while he and Xavier went to examine the body. It took only a few minutes before Xavier came out of the half-open door. For the first time since I'd known him, he looked, well, grim.

"He has bite marks, all right," Xavier said. "That means the academy's vampires will need to be included in the investigation."

My heart sank. "Isn't there someone in charge of the town's vampires?"

"Yes, there is, but we usually don't report crimes to their leader unless they're serious enough to be taken to the council," said Xavier. "Edwin will send a report and it's up to the vampire council whether they want to answer or not. The students, on the other hand—"

"Will be called in for questioning," said Edwin. "And your part in this, Aurora Hawthorn, is over."

I should be glad to hear it. It was time for me to hand the case over to the experts—and people who didn't wake up in a cold sweat every night after dreaming of vampires chasing them through the library. For my own sanity, I was best staying out of this one.

———

"I can't believe you didn't tell me you were going to *levitate* Swift out of here," Estelle said to Cass at the dinner table that evening.

"I told you I was releasing the beast into the sea today," she said indistinctly through a mouthful of potatoes.

"You said you planned to *transport* him out," said Estelle. "I thought you meant using a spell to directly send him into the sea. You live in a library with a thousand different possible ways of getting a kelpie into the water, and you pick the most dangerous one possible."

"Lighten up, Estelle," said Aunt Candace. "You're sounding positively middle-aged."

"And you dragged Rory into your ridiculous scheme, too," added Estelle.

"We already went over it," I said, not keen to see my family dissolve into yet another argument. Aunt Candace's floating pen and paper told a different story. "I'm not happy about it, but it's done."

"And will never happen again," added Aunt Adelaide. "From now on, it's time you made an effort to help the rest of us, Cassandra."

Cass rolled her eyes, and Aunt Candace looked up. "Are we going to start talking about the dead student yet? Because I have questions—"

"Didn't you get enough when you were snooping around eavesdropping on Edwin's questioning of the suspects?" Aunt Adelaide pushed her empty plate away. "Don't think I didn't see you."

Aunt Candace shrugged. "They were making no effort to lower their voices."

Aunt Adelaide tutted. "It's disrespectful. The poor boy."

"Didn't he get bitten by a vampire on purpose?" asked Cass.

"He did?" Estelle turned to her, a questioning look on her face.

"Yeah, all the students are saying so," said Cass, in smug tones. "They say he died by accident in a vampire transformation gone wrong."

"Nobody knows that for sure," I said. "Bite marks were found on his body, but he's definitely dead. Xavier said he'd be able to tell if he wasn't."

"Xavier said, did he?" Cass raised an eyebrow at me. "You're aware he's pretty much a zombie, right?"

"Cass, that's enough," said Aunt Adelaide. "There's

nothing wrong with Rory making friends. Especially as you took advantage of her earlier today."

"She agreed to help me!" Cass protested.

I put down my fork, not in the mood to argue about either Xavier or my misadventures with Cass. Even if I suspected Aunt Adelaide was right, and that Cass had talked me into it because I was the person least likely to say no.

"Want to head upstairs and watch a movie?" Estelle said, pushing her own plate away.

"Sure."

Relieved to escape Cass's snide remarks and the discussion of the murder, I rose to my feet and left the dining room.

"I'll make hot chocolate," said Estelle. "And maybe steal some of Mum's cake."

"Sounds good," I said, following her into the kitchen through the half-open door. "I could use some relaxation. How was class?"

"Compared to the day you had? Positively relaxing." She waved her wand and levitated a jar of cocoa out of the cupboard. "First Cass, then the Reaper. And you went with him to the police station?"

I lifted the box of cake from the cupboard and went to fetch some plates. "We had to check whether there were bite marks on the body in case he rose from the dead. I found out he checked out a beginner's guide to vampires from the library last week, which is why I thought he might have gone ahead with the transformation."

"Ah," she said. "Yeah, put together, those two things suggest he might have done it. Weird how his soul vanished, though. I'm sure the Reaper will sort it out."

"Yeah, I'm sure he will." For all our sakes, I really hoped so.

"I can't believe Cass, either." Estelle handed me a mug of delicious-smelling hot chocolate.

"I did try to tell her she was better off using a transportation spell," I said. "She wanted to say goodbye in person, I think."

Estelle blew on her hot chocolate to cool it. "She must like you a little to admit that."

"It was more inferred than implied," I said. "Anyway, the whole town knows after we made a spectacle in the town square. Not to mention in the lobby. I'm impressed all the water didn't damage the books."

"Oh, we've had worse than a kelpie on the loose in here," she said.

"From Cass?" I said. "She'll need a new pet project to replace Swift, I imagine, whatever Aunt Adelaide says."

There was a loud knocking sound from the library.

I turned to Estelle. "Expecting anyone?"

"No…" Estelle and I left our mugs and the cake behind, and we walked out into the short corridor connecting our living quarters to the main part of the library. Another knock sounded, loud in the otherwise silent and empty lobby.

The library was shrouded in darkness at this hour, lit only by the floating lanterns that appeared in the evenings. They gave it an eerie, atmospheric feel, and I jumped at the sight of a giant black bird sitting on the door frame.

"Jesus, Jet," I said. "I thought you were Poe's raven sent here to haunt us."

Jet cawed, fluttering out the way when Estelle opened the front door. A figure dressed in black holding a scythe greeted us.

"Hey there," Xavier said. "Sorry, I didn't want to barge in here after hours without knocking first."

"What're you doing here?" I asked, genuinely confused.

"I'm definitely not here to pick you up for a clandestine

meeting with the academy's vampire students before night classes start," he said, with a wink.

"Well, of course not," I said, a grin forming. "They have classes on Sundays?"

"The enthusiastic students do, which works in our favour," said Xavier, with a smile that made him look more angelic than ever. "Want to go?"

I looked at Estelle. "I take it that won't be a problem?"

Estelle pressed her lips together, but there was a glint of amusement in her eyes. "I'll tell my mum, and I'll keep your hot chocolate warm, okay?"

"Thanks." I turned to Xavier. "Let's go."

"I was hoping you'd say that." Xavier pushed the door open, and the Reaper and I walked out into the night.

4

To my surprise, Xavier took my arm to help me climb off the doorstep in the dark. Only for a few seconds, but long enough for an unexpected frisson of heat to spark through my entire body. Before I could scramble my thoughts together to speak, he'd let go. Shaking my head in an attempt to pull myself together, I jumped when a pair of beady yellow eyes looked at me from the darkness.

"Jet?" I let the crow land on my shoulder. "You want to come?"

"He can if he likes," said Xavier. "You won't be in any danger, though. These are teenage vampires, immature and impulsive."

"Are they more likely to have bitten Andrew than an adult vampire?"

"I'd say yes." Xavier resumed walking again, his footsteps hardly making a sound in the night. "As I said—immature and impulsive. An argument may have got out of hand, or a dare. Anything."

"And they tossed his body off the pier into the water?" I

wrapped my cloak tightly around me to keep off the chill. "Wait, why does the vampires' school take place at night? I thought vampires could walk around during the day just fine."

"They can," he said, "but they're more active at night. Most of them sleep at dawn, from what I heard. As I said, I don't generally interact with them."

"Yeah, I can't say I do either." I'd been avoiding Dominic when he came to visit my aunt—though more due to embarrassment at landing him in jail than fear of him biting me. "I assume they're expecting us?"

"Yes, they are, since I'm officially on the case," he responded. "The academy's this way."

I hadn't explored most of the town yet, especially at night. Lamps lit the winding streets, casting the stone cottages into darkness. The absence of normal transportation—regular cars didn't function well around magic—hadn't struck me as significant until now, but away from the library, the silence was so absolute that it seemed more like walking through a field in the middle of nowhere than through a town with a few thousand residents. The stars above appeared unusually bright, like tiny gemstones. I hadn't grown up in a big city, but I'd never seen them so clearly before.

We walked for about ten minutes until we came to a large brick building surrounded by high fences. The blinds were down, which would seem normal and not ominous if not for my knowledge that vampire class was in session.

Xavier paused outside the gate. "I can walk through, but you can't."

"You can walk through walls?" I blinked at him. "Is there anything you can't do?"

"Fly," he said, as Jet kicked off from my shoulder and took flight, leaving us standing outside. *Thanks for that, Jet.* I could technically use my biblio-witch magic to fly, too, but with an entire school of vampires potentially waiting on the other side of the gate, that would not be a wise idea. The space on the other side hid a dozen dark corners which might contain a vampire lying in wait to snag an unsuspecting human snack.

The gates creaked open, making me jump backwards.

Xavier caught my arm. "Relax, they're expecting us. Told you they were."

"No need to be smug." I followed him in, unnerved by how dark and creepy the academy looked at night. It probably resembled a typical school during the day, but in the shadows, its arched windows and dark corners looked like the perfect setting for a horror movie. I jumped again when a bat flew past. "Was that one of the vampires?"

"No," he said, sounding amused. "Is that from one of those stories from the normal world, vampires turning into bats?"

"In some stories," I said. "The 'needing an invitation to enter someone's home' rule turned out to be accurate. Though Mortimer Vale managed to get around that one."

Immediately, I regretted saying his name. He might be locked in a prison cell that even a vampire couldn't escape from, that didn't change the fact that two of his friends were at large, determined to get their hands on my dad's journal. That was one of the reasons I hadn't explored the town alone, aside from the dismal weather. Going further than the seafront wasn't usually necessary, and the library had everything I needed. I'd always considered myself necessarily cautious rather than a coward, but the way my heart jumpstarted at every sound set my teeth grinding.

Pull yourself together, Rory.

Xavier rang the buzzer by the front doors to the building, which opened by themselves.

"Is someone watching us?" I whispered.

"Quite possibly."

I looked for vampires lurking in the shadows, but they were so good at pretending to be statues that I could walk right past one and not notice. They also seemed to be able to see in the dark, judging by the barely-lit corridors. I walked close to Xavier to avoid tripping until he paused outside a classroom which had the curtains drawn. The murmur of voices came from within.

Xavier swore under his breath. "It sounds like we weren't the only ones who came here to speak with the vampires."

The door opened. I expected Edwin to confront us, but instead, a woman wearing a long black dress turned in our direction, then stepped towards the door with a speed that made my vision blur.

My body froze. The way she'd moved brought back all my bad memories. I wouldn't forget how those three vampires had toyed with me, hunting me like prey.

"I am Evangeline," said the woman. "It's an honour to meet you, Aurora Hawthorn."

Her voice was rich and smooth and almost made me overlook the pointed canines as she grinned at me. Her lips were painted blood red, her skin was the colour and texture of porcelain, and her hair cascaded down her back in dark curls. She looked like she'd stepped out of a textbook depicting the beginner's guide to vampirism—and I had the distinct impression she knew it. The woman regarded me as though I was more of a curiosity than a tasty snack, but I couldn't say it was much of an improvement. Vampires had super-sensitive hearing on top of their ability to read minds and move freakishly fast, so she'd probably listened to our whole conversation on the way in.

"We're here to speak to the students," said Xavier. "With permission. I'm guessing you did the same?"

Curious eyes watched us from waxwork faces within the classroom. Even the smaller children, the youngest around eleven or twelve, had the same eerie stillness. They also seemed to be dressed in all black, though maybe it was their school uniform. I wondered if any vampires rebelled against the norm and deliberately dressed in rainbow stripes or glitter to annoy their parents. Or if they took on unconventional jobs like a professional surfer or hairdresser. Halloween makeup artist, maybe. *How to be a walking corpse and still look drop-dead gorgeous... pun intended.*

The vampires all tilted their heads to look at me at once. Like creepy dolls. A shiver went down my spine. *Definitely shouldn't have come here.*

Evangeline closed the door behind her. "I think we should discuss the matter somewhere private. Not that it'll stop curious ears from listening in ... be careful what you think and say."

Of course. Nothing was private here. Even if the other vampires didn't follow and eavesdrop on us, they could read my thoughts, which meant they knew exactly how much I wished I was drinking hot chocolate with Estelle instead of being in this dark, freezing building in the middle of the night. Why had I talked myself into conquering my fears?

Evangeline led the way to an empty classroom and pushed open the door. Xavier and I entered the room as she pulled out a chair and sat in such an elegant manner that she made the drab leather chair look like a throne. Her dress left her pale arms bare and was completely unsuitable for the weather, but being a vampire, she wouldn't feel the cold.

"Evangeline is the leader of Ivory Beach's vampires," Xavier explained. "She's the first to know if there are any rogue vampires biting people."

Oh. That explained why Evangeline looked far more like a socialite than a schoolteacher. Then again, for all I knew, 'how to dress like you've stepped out of high society party' might be covered in the vampires' lesson plan. Mortimer Vale and his two friends had dressed the same way.

"You're here to help a friend," she observed, her gaze darting to Xavier. "Reaper… interesting. Am I to understand that one of your souls has been misplaced?"

"So it would seem," said Xavier. "Are you here to question the students about the unfortunate incident involving a student whose body showed up with bite marks in his neck?"

"Naturally," she said. "Since we're not currently aware of any rogues in town, then we assumed that the perpetrator was known to the victim."

"But the vampires go to night school and the humans go to school during the day, so how would they know one another?" I couldn't help asking.

She raised a perfectly plucked eyebrow at me. Did her eerie good looks come about as a by-product of vampirism or did only attractive people get bitten?

"Both genetics and the vampire virus, dear," she said.

Argh. *There's got to be a way to block her from reading my thoughts.*

"In answer to your question," she said, "it's clearly been a while since you were at school yourself, unless you weren't the rebellious type. Wouldn't a great number of teenagers find the idea of a secret night school for vampires… appealing?"

"Oh," I said. "Never thought of that. Of course they would." Except me, because I'd preferred to read fantasy adventures rather than paranormal romances when I was a teen. Admittedly, I hadn't been frightened of the idea of vampires until I'd met them for real.

"You didn't grow up in this world, of course," said Evangeline. "You were violently introduced to it, by a terrible encounter with three of my kin. I feel I must apologise for their appalling conduct."

"Oh." My cheeks heated. She must have seen my memories of the confrontation with Mortimer and the others the instant she saw me. What a first impression. "No worries. I know not all of you are like that."

She knew I was lying. Keeping a secret from a vampire was impossible. Maybe that's why they had to take separate classes, so vampires could learn the art of how to pretend not to notice when people had thoughts they disagreed with.

"We start with control early on," she said. "The first thing a new vampire learns to do is to filter the thoughts they pick up on from others. It's impossible to read multiple minds at once, so at first, it's very confusing to navigate."

"I see." She'd pulled half the questions I'd been thinking from my mind before they'd even formed. "That makes sense. So, uh, is anyone immune to mind-reading?"

"Him, for one," she said, indicating Xavier. "We can't read the minds of those who don't belong to the land of the living."

"What?" I turned to Xavier, who looked distinctly uncomfortable. "Oh, so that's why you're plucking out my thoughts and not his."

"Yours are unguarded," she said. "I apologise for my intrusion. I assumed that by accompanying him here, you knew the risks."

"She didn't expect to see you here, Evangeline," said Xavier. "Nor did I. Have you spoken to—or read the minds of —all the students here?"

"Yes, I have," she said. "None of them were responsible for biting Mr Lynch or helping him turn himself into a vampire. If he had such ambitions, he didn't confide them to any of the students present in this building."

"Oh." My shoulders slumped. I'd been so sure that the book on vampirism was a viable clue. Of course, there was no way for us to tell if *she* told the truth, but there seemed little point in her lying either. She had no stake in this... *bad choice of phrasing, Rory.*

Evangeline grinned, showing her teeth, and I shrank backwards. "Very amusing, dear."

She thought I was funny? That, or she was mocking me.

"Do you have any theories on who might have bitten Andrew before he died?" I asked hesitantly. "I assume you know I met three rogues before I came here, and two of them are still out there."

"If the other two were in town, I'd know about it," she said. "And this Mortimer Vale character remains behind bars, as is right."

"If that's all you have to tell us, we're grateful for the help," said Xavier.

"Of course. Always a pleasure talking to you, Reaper. Aurora, it's been delightful to meet you."

"Ah, you too," I said, standing hastily.

She glided to the door and was outside in a blink. I sucked in a breath and turned to Xavier. "I guess there's no point in speaking to the students, then."

I wasn't at all keen to go back in that classroom filled with creepy children who looked like living dolls anyway— and worse was knowing that *they* knew exactly what I thought of them.

"I think we'd have more luck talking to the living students." Xavier strode through the corridor to the exit, and I did my best not to glance at the classroom containing the vampires. Several more bats flew overhead, along with a crow who I mistook for Jet until it didn't stop to land on my shoulder.

"I'm not being unreasonable when I say I don't want to see another vampire for a while, am I?" I whispered to Xavier as we left the building.

"No, you're not," he said. "Sorry. I should have mentioned

my thoughts can't be read. It feels dishonest, especially when they invaded your privacy like that."

"I should have expected it," I said. "Wish I could block them from my thoughts. She said they can't read dead people's thoughts…"

"Ghosts," he said. "And Reapers. That's it, I think. I might be wrong. Like I said—not an expert. And it doesn't go both ways. Nobody can read *their* thoughts except other vampires, so they keep their secrets to themselves."

"That seems unfair." Though it wasn't like any of the other advantages vampires had were remotely fair, either. I appreciated Dominic's effort to minimise his use of mind-reading on me now I'd met the vampires' leader. "Evangeline isn't what I expected."

"That's what I thought, too," he said. "We've met a few times. Crossed paths."

"In dark graveyards at night?" I said. "I suppose you both deal with dead bodies. Yours just *stay* dead."

"Usually," he said.

I shuddered. "All right, that's enough night-time adventuring for me. I prefer my horror stories between the pages of books—and most of the time not even then."

"Good job you haven't found the horror section yet," he said.

"Thankfully." The library held a thousand surprises, and I'd only scratched the surface. "I guess you've been there before?"

"Once or twice," he said. "It's usually to look up things for my boss."

"Can't he come himself?" I asked. "I've never met him…"

"He prefers to keep an aura of mystery," he said. "That, and he has a reputation for being antisocial."

"And grim," I added. "Poor Andrew… I wish there was something we could have done."

"We tried," he said. "It would have caused a lot of trouble if one of the vampire students had been responsible for his death."

"I bet." I stopped walking when Jet landed on my arm. "What in the world have you been doing? Making friends with the vampires?"

The crow chirped.

"I wish I could understand him," I said to Xavier. "He and I are supposed to have a familiar bond, but he's friendly with everyone and he spends more time with Cass than he does with me. At least he did, when she was hiding the kelpie."

"I can't say familiars are my area of expertise either," Xavier said. "But maybe you'll start to cover that in your magic lessons soon."

"Aunt Adelaide did mention something about familiar training," I said. "But I don't know if it's for beginners or not. I haven't even passed my wand test yet."

Due to the academy closing for the school holidays soon, I wouldn't be able to take the test until January.

"You've been focused on your biblio-witch training, right?" he said.

"Yeah," I said. "Waving a wand is more complicated than simply writing a word in a book. Maybe I'll even catch up to your ability to walk through walls."

He grinned. "I can only do it when there's a soul I have to help. Which tends to be attached to a dead body, usually."

"That's one downside."

"I like to focus on the perks of the job," he said. "Pity the soul didn't disappear in the library this time. Then at least I'd have an excuse to spend time with you."

My heart missed a beat. He wanted to spend time with me? That... sounded almost like he thought we were on a date. Which we weren't. It went against the rules of being a Reaper, and I didn't want to get into trouble with his boss.

Meeting the vampires' leader was more than enough excitement for one night.

"Your boss won't make you swim around the ocean looking for a missing soul, will he?" I asked.

"Nah," he said. "From what I heard from the other students and Edwin, Andrew was last seen leaving his house to go to the library. So unless someone kidnapped him and took him further up the coast, he did die in this area. That means his soul should have been mine to reap. But it wasn't."

Then who took it?

5

Sylvester woke me up the following morning by singing "Rise and shine!" in my ear. I groaned and pulled the covers over my head. Who needed an alarm clock when you had a familiar who sang like a cat with its tail stuck in a washing machine?

Jet landed on my other side and chirped loudly in my ear.

"Really," I said to both of them. "That's not necessary. I'm coming."

I shoved the covers off and scrambled around looking for my clothes. Judging by the early hour, it was time for a magic lesson. I was supposed to be on an official timetable, but since Aunt Candace was the one in charge of most of my lessons, my timetable tended to follow the rule of 'whenever Aunt Candace isn't working on her manuscript'. Which usually meant first thing in the morning, because Aunt Candace required a pot of coffee to function.

So did I, come to that. My eyes were barely open by the time I'd tugged on my silver-lined cloak, dragged a brush through my hair, and grabbed my Biblio-Witch Inventory, pen and notebook. Shoving them into a bag along with my textbooks, I rushed out of my room and ran headlong into a brick wall.

"Ow!"

Stars danced before my eyes. Now thoroughly awake, I rubbed my forehead. Outside my door, there was supposed to be a corridor leading to the stairs. Instead, a solid brick wall filled the space, as though it had been displaced from somewhere outside. My head throbbed, and I felt a hideous bruise forming between my eyes. The library hadn't pulled a trick like that on me for a while, but I'd bet it was because Cass was still mad at me after yesterday. What had she expected me to do to stop the kelpie from running off, sing him a lullaby?

"I have to get to my lesson, if you don't mind," I said to the wall. "Can you please move?"

Being polite was usually the best way to handle the library. Sure enough, the wall obligingly slid to the side, revealing the path to the stairs. My forehead gave another throb, but I ignored it and picked up my bag.

The stairs let me climb down without collapsing, which was a mercy, and I found my way to the classroom on the ground floor. Aunt Candace sat at the front of the room with a pot of coffee on the desk and a heavy-looking textbook open in front of her.

"Goodness, what happened to your face?" said Aunt Candace. Beside her, her notebook and pen stirred as though hoping for a good story. "Did you find the martial arts section?"

"Nope, a random brick wall appeared outside my room," I said. "Can you please heal the damage? I don't need people thinking I've got into a fight."

"Well, I *suppose*." She pulled out her wand. "Now is a perfect time to demonstrate healing spells."

She waved her wand in a complicated motion and the

pain vanished from my forehead. Then she picked up a stick from her desk and handed it to me. "Copy what I just did."

I looked down at the stick of wood and held it up. "Er… can you show me again?"

She tutted. "That's not much use, is it? Show me."

I tried to copy her movement from memory. Aunt Candace rolled her eyes. "If that were a wand, you'd have disappeared my eyebrows."

"Can you show me it again?" I asked.

"I can't demonstrate it properly unless you injure yourself," she said. "Go on, I'll wait. I'm sure you can find a book to trip over."

"Please tell me you're joking." I never could tell with Aunt Candace. It didn't help that her notebook and pen were floating above her desk, recording our entire conversation.

And I wonder why I once suspected her of murder.

When she didn't reply, I waved my 'wand' again.

"Terrible," she said. "Left, not right, and try to put less power into it. You're healing an injury, not swinging a tennis racket."

"All right." I tried again, waving the wand slower this time.

Aunt Candace tutted. "If the wand were real, your fingers and toes would have switched places. Hmm. Maybe you should trial it with my wand—"

"What are you doing?" said Aunt Adelaide's voice from behind me. "Candace, don't tell me you're trying to force advanced spells on her already."

"I thought we'd go with the flow," answered her sister.

Aunt Adelaide sighed. "There's a syllabus, you know. And she has to pass the basic theory exam before she can own a wand. How far are you in the textbook?"

"I think we've covered a lot of ground," said Aunt Candace.

Aunt Adelaide strode across the room and picked up the textbook. "You covered the first ten pages and then skipped to chapter twenty-seven. Why? That's not on Rory's exam, Candace."

"I never said I was perfect."

"Don't worry, I read the whole thing in my spare time," I put in. "I can probably pass the exam..."

Aunt Adelaide looked over her shoulder at me. "Yes, I'm sure you can, but *really,* Candace. You can't expect her to grasp complex wand mechanics on the first attempt."

"I don't see why not," said Aunt Candace. "Anyway, as I said, I'm not a teacher. Isn't there an academy tutor with too much free time on their hands?"

"I've been looking for one, but it's close to the holidays," Aunt Adelaide said. "Can you try to stay on topic for the rest of the hour?"

"Yes, all right, all right," said Aunt Candace, looking disgruntled. "Turn back to the first chapter, then, Rory."

I left the classroom an hour later knowing more than I'd ever wanted to about underwater plants, but not much more about the basic wand movements. I went to the kitchen to make coffee, since Aunt Candace had declined to share any of hers with me, and found Aunt Adelaide had left me a mug next to a plate of buttered toast. I took them through to the living room and found my aunt tidying the contents of one of the cupboards on the sideboard. While my friends' families kept antique china in their cabinets, my new family stored their best potion-making gear in theirs.

"How'd it go?" she asked. "Let me guess—she went off on a tangent. What was this one?"

"Aquatic plants." I took a seat on the sofa and sipping my coffee. "It wasn't that bad. I had lecturers who used to do that when I was at university as well. We had to steer them back on topic otherwise they'd go off on one about their thesis and never get back to the subject at hand."

"We'll find you a tutor," she said, selecting a few polished instruments and placing them on the sideboard next to a large silver cauldron. "You'll be starting familiar training tomorrow, too—that'll be a nice change of pace for you."

I swallowed my bite of toast. "What, to teach Jet and me how to communicate?"

"Essentially," she said. "If you can do that, you might be able to skip a few grades in your magical education. It's a shame that you have to pass the theory exam before you can get a wand."

"I don't mind waiting," I said. "I have my biblio-witch magic. That's more than enough for now."

Just learning my way around the library was occupying enough of my brain space without adding wand lessons on top of it. Besides, wand-waving was much more complicated than the biblio-witch magic which had come naturally to me ever since it'd saved my life.

"I find wands can be more adaptable for practical use," she said. "But I understand why you would feel that the first magic you developed is the most intuitive. Estelle prefers biblio-witch magic. Cass, too. She rarely uses her wand."

"She rarely uses magic at all." Even with Swift rampaging around, she'd only used magic on him as a last resort. "Oh, except on the library. When will I learn to do that?"

"That's a combination of advanced biblio-witch magic and a level of trust between yourself and the library that can only develop over time," said Aunt Adelaide, locking the cabinet. "I know the basic lessons are frustrating, but they're laying a foundation for the rest of your magical development."

"I don't mind beginner's classes." With Aunt Candace in charge, I ended up walking away with a bunch of obscure facts on her latest obsession in addition to basic knowledge. "What's on the agenda for today?"

"There's a whole heap of returns to sort," she said. "Also, the students left the Reading Corner in a real mess yesterday. Most of them ended up leaving early after the unfortunate incident at the beach."

"Ah, yeah." To my relief, my aunt hadn't objected to my night-time excursion with Xavier, only told me to be careful not to annoy the vampires. "I can tidy it now, if you like."

"That'd be wonderful, Rory."

The last time I'd solved a murder, I'd found the clues right here in the library. I might not know where Andrew Lynch hung out in his free time, but his fellow students had been in the Reading Corner for hours yesterday. Maybe he wasn't the only person who'd taken a passing interest in vampires.

———

When I'd finished my breakfast, I headed to my favourite part of the ground floor, a space near the back filled with bean bags, cushions, hammocks and comfy seats. The Reading Corner was also the site of the weekly poetry night and various other functions. Yesterday's students had left empty crisp packets, scraps of paper, and even articles of clothing lying around. I sorted everything into two piles: 'lost property' and 'junk'. Then I added a third pile, 'ambiguous', for things like half-written essays and broken pens. It was a wonder any of them had walked out with anything they came in with. Shaking my head, I did a last circuit of the Reading Corner and spotted a piece of paper affixed to one of the shelves near the back.

'This is written in invisible ink', the poster said, which was clearly untrue. Above that, the heading said, 'Aspiring Vampires Society'.

Frowning, I read on. 'Each meeting is at six pm on Monday, while the Poetry Night is taking place. Come to the upper right corner of the library.'

Aspiring Vampires Society? Was that even allowed? And had Andrew Lynch been a member, before his untimely death?

I usually spent Poetry Nights marathoning Netflix with Estelle to avoid having to listen to the neighbourhoods' worst poets, but now I had a new plan: meet the Aspiring Vampires Society and find out if they were connected with Andrew's death.

———

By the time the Poetry Night rolled around, I was more in the mood to curl up and nap than deal with vampires—or wannabe-vampires, for that matter. The brick wall incident was only the beginning, and after a day of false turns, fake doors, disappearing floors and books that spat slime at me when I picked them up, I had a pounding headache and the strong desire to lock Cass in the vampire's basement for a bit.

Estelle found me waiting in an alcove near the Reading Corner as the various attendees of the poetry night filed into the library. "Are you joining in the poetry night?"

"Definitely not," I said. "I'm waiting for the Aspiring Vampires Society members to show their faces."

"The *what?*" asked Estelle.

"I found this earlier," I said, showing her the poster I'd removed from the shelf. "They're supposed to be meeting at the same time as the poetry night, in the back corner of the library. Seems more than a coincidence, considering what happened to Andrew."

"Huh," she said. "Yeah, you're right. It's worth checking out."

"I won't last five minutes at the poetry night, besides," I added. "I don't blame that wizard last week for sneakily casting a sneezing spell on half the audience to get the guy with the twenty-page dramatic poem to stop."

She grinned. "We can watch a movie once we've dealt with the vampires."

"They're not real vampires." I dropped my voice as a group of wizards wearing green cloaks filed into the Reading Corner. Oddly enough, the poetry night had gained popularity after two people had died a few weeks ago, and every night brought at least one performance inspired by the events of my arrival here in Ivory Beach. That was reason enough to avoid them. One thing Aunt Candace and I had in common—we weren't fond of being the centre of attention.

The crowd filled the Reading Corner, gathering in every available chair and hammock. Then a croaking noise sounded as the first poet took to the stage. A tall red-haired wizard unfurled a roll of paper. He carried a toad tucked under one arm, for some inexplicable reason. "Today, I'm here to read my—"

As he started his recital, the toad jumped out of his hands and hopped away among the shelves.

"Toad on the loose!" someone yelled.

The wizard dived to catch his toad, missed, and crashed headlong into the snack bar, knocking sandwiches flying. The toad disappeared between two shelves at an impressive speed.

Estelle groaned. "I'll deal with them. You find those aspiring vampires. Let me know if you need backup, okay?"

"Will do." They couldn't be as scary as the vampires' actual, genuine leader, right? They were just a bunch of kids. *I think.*

I ducked behind the shelves at the back of the library, searching for the meeting point. The shelves here formed a maze that was difficult to navigate even without the library pranking me, so I followed the faint sound of voices that weren't screaming about toads until I found a gap in the shelves.

About ten or so young men and women had gathered in the corner around a desk that'd clearly been pulled out from one of the classrooms. A teenage boy of around sixteen stood on the desk, holding a clipboard. He wore a hooded cape that looked like it was designed for someone a foot taller than him, and when he bared his teeth at me, the canines were pointed. He took a step forwards, tripped off the table, and landed flat on his face.

My apprehension vanished. Real vampires didn't trip or stumble. They didn't blush, either. His face was bright red when he came upright. "What are you doing here?"

"I'd like to have a word with you about this." I held up the poster.

"How did you read the invisible ink?" he demanded.

"It's not invisible," I said, showing the words to the other students. "See?"

So much for interrupting a dangerous group of potential murderers.

He whirled on a fellow student, a tall black boy with dreadlocks. "I told you to use the invisible ink, Zach."

"No, you didn't," said the boy. "Besides, how's anyone meant to know the meeting time if the ink's invisible?"

"Night vision," he said.

"I don't have night vision yet, Nick," he protested.

"Hang on," I said, wondering what in the world I'd wandered into. "I'll leave you to your meeting if you answer a couple of questions. That's all I want."

"What questions?" the leader pushed his hair into place,

revealing it was actually a black wig, sitting at a lopsided angle on his forehead. I choked back a laugh.

"I wanted to know if Andrew Lynch was a member of your group," I said. "That's all."

"Yes," said the guy with dreadlocks who he'd called Zach. "He was. Gail talked him into joining, right?"

A red-haired girl with freckles and a ponytail gave him a furious glare. "Before we broke up, yes, I did. But I had nothing to do with his death. None of us did."

"Back up a second," I said. "You meet every week... to discuss how to turn yourselves into vampires? Is that right?"

"No," said the guy in the cape. His fake fangs popped out of his mouth as he spoke and he hastily shoved them in again. "We meet to discuss the merits of being one of the living dead."

"That's the same as what I just said."

"No, it isn't," he said, his voice slightly muffled by the lopsided fangs. "I meant in a theoretical sense."

I blinked. "What, and the cape and the fangs are just an aesthetic?"

"Why not?" Giving up on the fangs, he pulled them out of his mouth and set them down on the table. "Vampires get all the best stylistic options. We're trying to be the best vampires we can be *without* all that immortality nonsense."

I spotted the clipboard he'd dropped when he'd fallen off the table and picked it up. "Curriculum. Day 1: night vision classes. Turn off lights and wander around. Day 2: drinking blood. May use juice as a substitute. Day 3: vampire dance lessons." I stopped reading, biting my tongue before I burst out laughing.

The vampires' esteemed leader flushed to his hairline. "Stop making fun of us!"

"I'm not," I lied. "I'm just trying to figure out how Andrew went from coming to these meetings to showing up dead in the sea with bite marks in his neck. Actual bite marks, I mean, not... those." I gestured at the fake fangs, which looked like the sort of plastic Halloween costume you could get from a fancy dress shop in the normal world.

Several of the students exchanged glances. "Maybe he did go ahead and do it," said Zach. "He was always acting weird, moody..."

I decided not to point out that the above description applied to everyone in this very corner. "Did he start drinking blood, or only coming out at night?"

"He took part in all of our lessons," said the leading Aspiring Vampire. "I dunno, I wouldn't have noticed if he'd done it for real."

Very helpful. How was I supposed to work out if he was actually a vampire if he'd been pretending to be one for weeks before he'd turned? *If* he'd turned?

"Okay, can I have a word with you alone?" I indicated the redheaded girl. "I know you probably spoke to the police, but I'm guessing they don't know about this meeting. If you'd prefer it to stay that way, then I'd like you to answer my questions."

The girl looked frightened. Maybe I'd been a bit harsh. But after the day I'd had, the last thing I needed was to end up letting a murderer slip away. I'd nearly done the same a few weeks ago, and I had no desire for the wrong person to wind up jailed again.

The girl walked with me to an alcove between shelves. "What do you want to ask?" she asked. "I already told the police I didn't do it."

"You said you and Andrew broke up?" I asked her. "If you don't mind my asking, why?"

She grimaced. "We had issues for a while. We just grew apart."

Hmm. "So you're the one who talked him into joining the group?"

"Yeah." She looked down. "I wish I hadn't. He wasn't into the whole vampire thing originally. But it seemed like a bit of harmless fun. The vampires *do* get all the cool tricks. It's not like any of us planned to get ourselves bitten and turned. I know how it all works and I don't want to live forever. Andrew didn't either, but—he didn't want to die." Her voice broke. "I blamed Nick, but it's my fault for talking him into joining. I don't know what he was thinking."

If she told the truth, it was possible that he'd sought out a vampire to bite him, and then somehow botched it. That seemed as likely as anything else. But then, where had his soul ended up? These kids likely wouldn't know, if even the Reaper didn't.

"Okay," I said. "Thanks for answering my questions."

The sound of yelling had quietened from behind the shelves, suggesting that the toad had been caught and order restored to the poetry night. I walked back to the Aspiring Vampires' corner, where Nick had put his clipboard away.

"I think we should break this meeting up for now," he said. "Wait to hear from me—*with* the invisible ink this time, Zach. Where is it?"

"I dunno, I had it here in the library, I swear."

"Don't forget to pick up all your possessions," I said to the group, before heading back the way I'd come. Nick scowled after me, but nobody moved to challenge me.

Costumes aside, none of them behaved remotely like vampires at all. If they hadn't wanted to be found out, they might have picked somewhere to hold their gathering other than the town's most popular meeting location. They struck me as almost entirely harmless... and yet Andrew was still dead.

Maybe I should have asked the girl more questions. Now I thought back, I was sure she and the boy on the desk had been the two who'd got into a fight in the library when the police had come to report Andrew's murder. Why? She'd blamed Nick for his death, but that didn't mean he was directly responsible.

But had the society led to Andrew's death? Or had it only been a symptom of his fascination with vampires?

6

After breakfast the following morning, Aunt Adelaide asked me to meet her downstairs for my first familiar training session. I walked into the classroom to find a disgruntled-looking Cass waiting at the front desk besides Aunt Adelaide.

"Wait, Cass is my tutor?" I looked at my aunt in disbelief.

"Well, nobody else was free," said Aunt Adelaide apologetically. "And she has the strongest bond with Sylvester out of all of us."

"Because she always gives me treats," Sylvester said. "Candace doesn't even know my name."

"There it is," said Cass, wearing her sourest expression. "Lesson one: know your familiar's name. Call him and he'll come."

"I know how to do that," I said. *"You* know that. You've seen me do it."

"Yeah, but for the purposes of this *lesson—*" she gave her mother a disgruntled look—"I have to ask you to demonstrate."

"Jet," I said. "Come here."

There was a pause, then the little crow flew into the classroom to land on my shoulder.

"That's lesson one," said Cass, moving towards the door. "Come back next week for part two—"

Aunt Adelaide blocked the way. "You know what Rory has already covered. I'm sure you can take an hour from your busy schedule to teach her the rest of the first chapter."

"I'm not a teacher," Cass retaliated. "Besides, it's all there in the textbook."

"I'll read it myself," I said. "It's not a problem. I'd prefer to do it that way."

If this was what Cass was like as a teacher with supervision, I'd rather not find out what she'd be able to do without anyone watching. Order Sylvester to annoy me all day, probably.

Aunt Adelaide released a breath. "You aren't off the hook, Cass. You're cleaning the third-floor corridor. There's been a flood."

Cass scowled. "I'd rather take the lessons."

"Too late," I said, approaching the door. Aunt Adelaide didn't stop me. "I'm going to go and read for a bit. So long, Cass."

I gave her a little wave as I walked out. I'd probably pay for this one in a hundred pranks from the library, but it was worth it to see her face fall. I'd much rather self-teach from the familiar textbook than deal with an hour of Cass's complaints, snide comments and practical jokes. It wasn't like reading books was a punishment for me in the slightest.

Sylvester's raucous laughter followed me as I walked to the Reading Corner, found a spare chair, and sat down to read. The chair collapsed, sending me sprawling onto my back. *Really, Cass.* Climbing to my feet, I spotted a cloak someone had left behind in the corner, either from the poetry night or from the wannabe-vampires' meeting. Now I looked closely, there were all sorts of random items scattered around. Apple cores. Homework. Socks.

I was starting to understand why librarians didn't get much actual reading done. By the time I'd sorted everything into piles, it was almost opening time. Tipping the junk into the bin, I checked the first lost property item, the dark cloak I'd found in the corner. The name label inside the hood read: *Andrew Lynch.*

Had someone borrowed his cloak? Or had he left it in here before he died? There was no badge like I saw on the academy students' uniforms, so it must be his 'vampire' costume. I turned it over and spotted a dark stain near the hem.

My heart jumped into my throat. The dark colour hid stains and it might have been anything, even water. But when I touched it, my hand came away red.

I started upright when the door opened, the sound carrying through the quiet library. Standing, I moved the pile of lost property, cloak included, and left them beside the front desk to deal with later.

I didn't get a spare moment until after lunch, in the hour or so before the after-school classes began. I took the opportunity to check the library's record book to see whether anyone other than Andrew had checked out the book on vampires recently. Before Andrew, it appeared the book had remained in the library for at least a few weeks. Then again, the group's meetings took place in the library, they didn't have to check any of the books out to use them in their meetings. I closed the record book and looked up to see Estelle approaching with an armful of books.

"How're you doing, Rory?"

"Suspiciously well." Well enough to suspect that Aunt Adelaide had guessed Cass had been using the library's magic against me, because no more pranks had hit me all morning.

That, or she'd been too occupied cleaning up the flood. I'd spotted her walking around dripping wet when I'd gone up to the third floor to return a book to the Magical Creatures Division earlier, and while she'd glared daggers at me, she hadn't tried anything else.

"Good," said Estelle. "I heard Cass flaked out on your familiar lesson this morning. Where is she?"

"Up on the third floor, dealing with a flood."

"Oh, that's where she's been all day," said Estelle. "I assumed she found a new guy. Or kelpie."

"I take it Swift never came back to say goodbye?" I said. "That's why she's still in a mood with me. I prefer studying on my own, so I don't mind that she didn't want to teach me. Pretty sure she and Sylvester would have ganged up on me."

"You might be right," she said, spotting the lost property box on the desk. "What's in there?"

"All the junk I found in the Reading Corner." I pulled out the cloak. "This is Andrew Lynch's. Guess he left it here before he died."

Estelle frowned at the label. "Oh. Should we give it to one of the other students to hand over to his family?"

"One thing first." I showed her the stain at the hem. "Can you figure out what that stain is? It turned red when I touched it."

She grimaced. "Please tell me you're not channelling Aunt Candace."

"It might help the police investigate."

"I knew it." She rolled her eyes. "Yes, I can do a detection spell on it. But after that, we're giving it back to Andrew's family, okay?"

"Of course," I said. "Thanks. I knew there must be a spell, but I didn't want to try anything too advanced."

"I think you could handle it," she said. "I know my mum wants to do everything by the book, but you don't have to.

Not that I'm recommending going as wild as Aunt Candace, but I think it's worth taking a few risks now and then."

Maybe she was right. I did have a tendency to play it safe —as safe as it was possible to in the magical world anyway.

As Estelle left, the members of the Aspiring Vampires Society all entered at the same time. While none of them wore their ridiculous costumes, they walked in a tight-knit group, whispering to one another. Wishing I had an eaves-dropping spell, I watched them pass, heading to the Reading Corner. Maybe they were discussing a new meeting spot for their group. They'd be hard-pressed to find anywhere open outside the library because almost all the town's social events took place here.

Inspiration struck.

"Hey, Sylvester," I said.

The owl flew over a moment later, landing on the desk next to me in a flutter of wings. "What is it? Need me to tie your shoelaces?"

"There's no need for that, Sylvester," I said. "Did you see those students who just came in? Would you be able to follow them and eavesdrop on their conversation?"

"Would I *what?*" he said. "I have never been so insulted in my life. I am an intelligent creature, not a spy."

"Spies are intelligent." His voice was so loud that I worried the students might overhear. "It's not just for me. Xavier—"

"Oh, your Reaper," he said. "Can't he find his own souls?"

"He's not mine—and that's not what it's about. The police would be grateful for any information on the murder—"

"Murder!" I winced at how loudly his voice echoed. "Obstructing a police investigation on top of being a disgrace to witchery. To think you want to accuse those nice academy students of committing a hideous crime. I should tell them."

"Don't!" I said, reaching out. He lunged at me with his

talon in answer, and I yanked my hand out of the way. "Ow! What's wrong with you?"

He huffed and took flight in a rustle of feathers, narrowly missing snagging my cloak in the process.

All right, then. If Sylvester refused to cooperate, then I'd just ask my own familiar for help.

"Hey, Jet," I called.

After a pause, the little crow flew down to land on the front desk, nudging my hand affectionately with his beak. I gave him a stroke along his glossy black feathers.

"Jet, can you do me a favour?" I asked. "I think those students—the ones who just came in—might be talking about Andrew Lynch, the guy who died last weekend. Would you be able to listen in on their conversation?"

Jet cawed, dipped his head, and took flight. Sorted. Okay, I couldn't actually understand him when he tried to talk to me, but I'd find a way to learn if he'd overheard anything useful later.

Despite what the students told me yesterday, I was sure they'd omitted details about Andrew's involvement in the Aspiring Vampires Society. If Andrew had gone ahead and transformed into a vampire for real, people would have noticed. It wasn't the sort of thing you could easily hide.

Besides, if they were as subtle as they'd been with their meeting, they wouldn't be hard to eavesdrop on.

Jet flew back over after about half an hour and landed on the open record book, nudging my fingers with his beak. I obligingly gave him a stroke.

"Did you hear anything from them?"

The crow let out a series of incomprehensible chirps.

"Uh, sorry, I don't understand. Can you give a demon-stration?"

He flapped his wings and flew around in circles, chirping. Maybe I should have learned how to communicate with him *before* telling him to spy on them. But even the most talented witches couldn't actually talk to their familiars. Sylvester was an exception.

I pulled out the familiar textbook and opened it, skipping the basics. While there didn't seem to be a listed spell that would enable me to understand his speech, I had no trouble getting Jet to follow my commands, though judging by the textbook's opening chapters, that wasn't always the case for a new witch. I felt a rush of gratitude that I had such a placid and friendly familiar who didn't make life difficult for me. Okay, Sylvester was a different story, but he was my family's familiar, not mine.

How can he talk, then? Okay, I was in a magical library that defied the laws of nature. You'd think by now I'd have learned not to ask that question.

"Hello," said Sylvester's voice. He landed on the desk in front of me as though my thoughts had conjured him up. "Not cheating by jumping ahead in the textbook, are you?"

"It's not cheating if I've already covered the basics," I pulled the textbook out of reach of the owl's talons. "Have you changed your mind and decided to help me after all?"

"Of course not," he said. "But if you're hoping that crow will be able to tell you anything useful, you'll be disappointed."

"Why, can *you* understand him?" I asked curiously.

"No," he said, with a sniff. "Unintelligent beings like him are beneath me."

Jet gave an indignant chirp.

"How did you learn to talk, anyway?" I asked.

"Cass," he said. "She used a familiar bonding spell. It was supposed to make her be able to understand me, but because I belong to the entire family, the spell was extended."

"Really?" I said. "Can I use the spell on Jet to make it so that I can understand his speech?"

"You *could,* but that would mean bending the rules." His eyes gleamed. "Not defying your aunt, are you?"

"I'm not defying anyone," I said. "She didn't tell me I couldn't do it. Besides, I can make up my own mind."

"Ooh," said Sylvester. "Very well, then, work your magic, Aurora dearest."

I glanced at Jet, who continued to pace around the desk, chirping. "Okay, where exactly do I find this spell? It's not in the familiar textbook."

"Of course it isn't," Sylvester said. "It's far too advanced for you. You don't even have a wand yet."

"No, but the familiar textbook only covers regular witch-craft," I said. "Is there a biblio-witch spell that does the same thing? Is that what Cass used?"

"Maybe." He landed directly in front of me, making me take an uneasy step back away from his sharp claws. "Are you sure you want to do this?"

Well... not really. But Jet had something to say about the students' discussion of the murder. Besides, I wouldn't lie, the idea of a sidekick only I could communicate with was appealing. That's what a familiar was supposed to be, right? And if it helped us find out who'd killed Andrew, so much the better.

"I'm sure," I said. "What's the spell, then?"

"What indeed? You'll have to ask your cousin."

"Come on, Sylvester, I know you know."

"I most certainly do not," he said, ruffling his feathers. "I didn't ask for the spell to be used on me, and I doubt your cousin meant it to be permanent."

"Go on," I said. "There must be somewhere in the library I can find the spell, right?"

"There *might.*" He rotated his head all the way around, in a manner that made me slightly nauseated to watch. "You're not trying to get into the *forbidden* room, are you?"

"Forbidden?" I frowned. "I thought Aunt Adelaide consulted the library all the time. Asking questions isn't forbidden, is it?"

"*She* consults the library for answers," he said. "It's beyond your level."

"Try me," I said, feeling an unexpected burst of annoyance. "What is the forbidden section?"

"The question room," he said, in a dramatic whisper. "It will answer any question at all, but at a price."

"Stop messing with me, Sylvester."

"I'm telling the truth, Aurora dearest," he said. "The question room *will* answer your questions, if you can find your way in. As for my warning, if you try to access magic beyond your level, it's capable of turning a lesser witch into a gibbering wreck."

"The familiar spell isn't that high-level, right?" I said, already having second thoughts. Sylvester's advice usually came with a catch even if he *didn't* give me advance warning. But if this room could answer any question, could it tell me who the murderer was?

"No, it isn't," said Sylvester. "I suppose you're too cautious to try it. The question room is for people who are brave enough to face their fears rather than hiding from vampires behind bookshelves and jumping at shadows."

"Hey!" I said indignantly, my face flushing. "You'd be scared of them too if you didn't have wings. How do I get into this question room, then?"

"The book, of course," he said. "Haven't you seen it? You walk past it every day."

"Might have escaped your attention, but we're in a library. I walk past a thousand books every day."

He tutted. "Someone's in a feisty mood. The book of questions is somewhere in that disorganised pile over there, because *someone* set a kelpie loose and messed up the entire ground floor."

"Oh." I scanned the area and spotted a pile of books I hadn't had the chance to return to the shelves yet. From examining the spines, it seemed they were the books that'd got knocked out of place during the kelpie's escape and had yet to be returned to their proper places. I moved each book aside until I found the plain black-covered book that had hit me with its vine-shaped defence mechanism when I'd tried to pick it up. "It's not going to attack me like last time, is it?"

"Relax, it's dormant," said Sylvester. "It won't bite."

"It's more the thorns I'm worried about." I hesitantly picked up the book and turned it over, but no thorny vines swiped at me this time. Its black leathery cover was blank, except for a silver question mark on the spine. "Which section does it go in?"

"The section is inside the book." Sylvester dropped his voice dramatically again.

"Uh... excuse me?

"The section it belongs in is inside the book," he said again, his feathers rustling.

I lowered the book. "How is that possible?"

"You've been here for weeks and you're still acting as though this place conforms to the simple rules you brought with you from the normal world?" He laughed, an echoing cackle. "Ask to enter the forbidden room, and the book shall oblige. Fair warning, though—you're only allowed to ask one question a day, and the room itself chooses whether to answer you or not."

Jet gave a warning chirp, but my curiosity was officially piqued. I turned the book over again, and a faint shimmer crossed the question mark symbol as it caught the light. As an avid reader, the idea that an entire world could exist between the pages wasn't a foreign one to me, but caution reared its head. Diving headfirst into an unknown book on the instructions of a mischievous familiar wasn't something the Rory who'd grown up in the normal world would do.

Then again, those simple rules I'd lived by had unravelled before my eyes. I was someone else now. Maybe someone who was willing to take a leap of faith to get the knowledge I needed.

"Having second thoughts, dear?" Sylvester said. "Not afraid you'll run into another vampire sleeping in a coffin?"

Annoyance at the owl's mocking fuelled my resolve. "No, I'm going in."

Even if I got lost, I had the piece of emergency paper in my pocket marked with a spell which would summon my aunt to my rescue. Never mind what Sylvester said. I was done playing it safe.

"Excellent." He shuffled to the edge of the desk. "You say, *I wish to enter the forbidden room,* and voila." He clicked his beak, making a noise which sounded like fingers snapping. "Go on, get on with it, then."

"Keep your feathers on." I opened the book and looked at the blank pages. "I wish to enter the forbidden room," I said.

The plain yellowed pages warped before my eyes, like distorted glass. Then my head pitched forwards, and I was falling.

Empty space unfolded, the colour of the yellowed pages. Dizziness swept my body as a weightless feeling took hold, my cloak swirling around my ankles. The book was no longer in my hands, and my arms flailed, searching for something to grab onto. Just as I sucked in air to scream, my feet hit soft carpet and my knees buckled.

I'd landed in a small square room with black-painted walls which had the same leathery texture as the book. My heart hammered so hard I felt it in my throat, while my arms wrapped around myself. Taking in a few quick breaths, I straightened upright. "So, uh, what now?"

No response.

"Okay… do I just ask my question?" I turned on the spot, looking for a prompt, but all four walls were the same shiny black as the floor and ceiling. Worse, my cloak felt lighter than usual. A swift check of my pockets confirmed my pen, notebook and Biblio-Witch Inventory were all gone, as though they'd been left behind when I'd entered the book. And though I didn't quite dare check and confirm it, the piece of parchment with the library's emergency words was probably absent, too. This wasn't the library at all. It was somewhere else entirely.

Calm down, Rory. If I asked my question, I should be allowed to leave, right? Sylvester might be a prankster, but he'd never knowingly put me in danger. Aunt Adelaide would never let him.

Taking in another deep breath, I said, "Here's my question: who murdered Andrew Lynch?"

There came the sound of a thunderclap, then the floor collapsed. A roaring wind crashed into me, hitting me full in the face. I fell into emptiness, my hands flailing once again— then everything went black.

A moment later, I came to, lying on my back behind the library's front desk. Jet fluttered over me, making alarmed twittering noises. Even Sylvester looked distinctly ruffled.

"You fool!" he howled. "You moronic turnip."

"Are you just going to keep calling me names rather than helping me up?" I struggled upright, my head pounding. My entire body hurt, like I really had fallen through a torrent of nothingness and crash-landed on the floor. "All I did was ask it who the killer was. Thanks for the help."

"I can't help you in there, you inept toadstool," said

Sylvester. "It's one of the parts of the library that's off-limits to familiars. Lucky for that crow of yours, really."

I grimaced, climbing to my feet. That'd teach me to dive into situations headfirst—literally—without considering the consequences. Since I hadn't had any of my magical props on me, I was lucky the room had let me out in one piece.

Maybe I should have just asked the room how to make myself able to communicate with Jet, like I'd planned. Now I'd wasted my chance.

"You'll have to try again tomorrow," said the owl. "One question per day."

Yeah, that's not happening. I'd almost rather face a class of teenage vampires than set foot in that room again.

I'd just have to find out how to speak to Jet the normal, non-risky way. Come to think of it, if Cass had used biblio-witch magic to make Sylvester able to talk, then it would be recorded inside her own Biblio-Witch Inventory. I could just borrow it when her back was turned. Much less hazardous than diving into the room of questions again.

Then I thought of Cass's furious expression when I'd run into her on the third floor. Perhaps not. Oh, well. What if it turned out Jet was secretly muttering insults about me? I didn't need two snarky familiars following me around.

"Rory!" Estelle rushed over to the front desk, looking panicked. "You weren't paranoid. It's blood, all right. And it's his cloak, too."

"What? Andrew's?"

She nodded, her mouth pinching. "I don't know if any of the other students are his friends, but we can ask them to take it back to his family."

"Or we can go in person," I suggested. "We can get the library book back while we're at it, too."

Jet would have to wait. It would be easier to talk to

Andrew's family in person than try to wrangle answers from a crow, anyway.

"How'd I guess you'd say that?" She folded the cloak over her arm. "Sylvester?"

The owl swooped down. "What is it now?"

"Fetch Cass and ask her to watch the front desk. We have an urgent errand to run."

"Urgent?" he said. "A likely story."

"Yes, it is," said Estelle. "Don't be difficult. Why are you in such a contrary mood today, anyway?"

"She can tell you," Sylvester said, jerking his head at me. "All right, fine. I will inform your mother of your daring quest."

Estelle raised an eyebrow at me. "What happened this time? Cass?"

"Not quite," I said. "I'll tell you on the way."

7

I recounted today's adventures as Estelle and I walked through the town square and turned down the main high street. While it'd been dark and sinister-looking at night, during the day it had the more ordinary appearance of a quirky village high street lined with shops selling all the magical necessities. The sweet smells of the magical sweet shop mingled with the burning scent of incense from a shop on the corner, underlaid by the less pleasant scents of bitter herbs from the local apothecary. Bright clothes filled one window beside a shop selling gold-plated cauldrons, and on the other side, the pleasant smell of flavoured coffee drifted from a small café.

"Aunt Adelaide will give me grief for going into the question room, won't she?" I asked.

"I won't mention it to her," said Estelle. "You know, when I said you might want to try something new, I didn't mean... that."

"It's not your fault. I shouldn't have let Sylvester get to me." I stepped aside to avoid a gaggle of witches laden with packages from the sweet shop. "And I should have just asked the question I originally wanted to ask and figured out how to make myself able to understand Jet."

"What, like Sylvester?" she asked. "Hmm. There *are* spells, but you'd need—"

"A wand. I know. Sylvester implied Cass used biblio-witchery to do it, which I *can* do. But he said he didn't know what she wrote."

"He might have been telling the truth," said Estelle. "It happened when I was a teenager, and Cass wouldn't tell me how she did it either. We just woke up one day and Sylvester could talk. He's been here since before I was born and knows the library backwards, so it didn't make a huge difference to his job, but he definitely became more difficult to handle afterwards."

"Hmm. Is that likely to happen with Jet?"

"Probably not," she said. "He's yours, which means he won't become attached to someone else, like Sylvester did with Cass. He refuses to let any of the rest of us use familiar spells on him. But Jet chose you already, so you should be able to do all the spells with enough practise if he's eager to learn."

"He is," I said. "I sent him to spy on the Aspiring Vampires in the library today, but since I can't understand anything he says, I have no idea if he overheard anything incriminating. That's why I wanted a communication spell."

"Oh." Her eyes sharpened with understanding. "That makes sense. I'll see if there's a spell which might work when we get back to the library."

We turned right into a narrow road lined with terraced houses. As we did so, a young man walked out of the gate on our right. He wore the academy's uniform and had longish blond hair.

"Is that Andrew's house?" said Estelle.

"Oh, yeah, it is," he said. "I was just leaving."

"You're from the academy, right?" I asked him. "And you knew Andrew."

"We were friends," he said. "I'm Cameron. I was just here with his family. I wanted to do what I could."

"I'm sorry for your loss," said Estelle.

"Yeah." He blinked a couple of times, though his eyes looked dry. "I never expected it, you know?"

I hesitated. "Do you... if it's okay to ask, do you know what may have happened the day he died?"

"I'm sorry, I don't," he said. "He was acting oddly for a while, though. Skipping school, that kind of thing."

"Really?" I said. "Did you hear he was a member of a secret club of students who admired vampires?"

"Even you know about it?" He shook his head. "Yeah, he was, for a few weeks. It's all he would talk about."

"Were you part of the club, too?" asked Estelle.

"No, but he tried to talk me into it," he said. "I was going to join, but now I guess not."

"You wanted to join? Why?" I asked.

He shrugged. "Vampires have an advantage over the rest of us. Why shouldn't we want to be more like them?"

Hmm. "Did Andrew think the same? How long was he a member?"

"A few weeks," Cameron said. "To be honest, I'm sure someone in that club must have had something to do with his death. He was fine before he joined up with them, and now..."

"But the group's purpose isn't about actually turning into a vampire, is it?" I said. "That's not the impression I got, anyway. They had night vision classes and stuff like that. And the guy who runs it definitely isn't a vampire."

"No, he's not," said Cameron. "But Nick and Andrew argued the day before he died."

"They did?" I frowned. "And then he showed up dead with bite marks in his neck. Nick can't have been responsible."

"I don't know what to think," Cameron said, glancing over his shoulder at Andrew's house. "Like I said, he was fine before he started getting involved in that club. I think he only joined as a joke at first, too. Then he started taking it super seriously. Complaining at me for wanting to hang out when he was in meetings. Acting moody. His girlfriend ditched him last week and he didn't even seem to care."

Estelle elbowed me in the ribs, alerting me to a curtain fluttering in the window. Andrew's parents must have spotted us.

"Thanks for talking to us," I said to Cameron. "If you find out anything else, you're welcome to come to the library and tell me in confidentiality."

"Oh, of course." He continued to walk, while I turned over his words in my mind. Nick couldn't have turned Andrew into a vampire by biting him even if they'd argued. So where had the bite marks come from?

Estelle turned to me. "The kid from the Aspiring Vampires Society? Did he really seem like a murderer?"

"No," I said. "He fell off a desk when I surprised him. Doesn't exactly have the vampire stealth thing going for him."

The guy couldn't even use invisible ink right. I doubted he'd committed the murder. I understood why Cameron would think so, though, given the circumstances. I'd see if Andrew's parents said any different before jumping to conclusions.

Estelle knocked on the door, which opened after a pause. Andrew's parents looked rough, as I'd expected. Both of them had dark circles under their eyes and looked at us with blank expressions.

"Hey," I said. "Sorry to bother you. We're from the library, and we wanted to return something of your son's we found."

Estelle held out the cloak. "I'm terribly sorry for your loss."

Mrs Lynch took it with trembling hands. "Thanks for returning it to us."

"I hope it's okay to ask, but we had it on record that he checked out a book called *A Novice's Guide to Vampirism.* Do you have it?" I asked.

"Oh." She looked over her shoulder, distracted. "I'm sure it's somewhere in his room... I haven't been in there since."

"I'll get it," said his father, not looking much keener on the idea.

"We can fetch it," Estelle said quickly. "I promise we won't touch anything."

Estelle was probably acting out of kindness, not just nosiness, but I couldn't help wondering if Andrew had left any clues behind. Not that I wanted to bother his grieving family, but if Andrew had been involved in that secret vampire society and ended up dead because of it, the police needed to know in case the same happened to others, too. If I jumped ahead and told them without proof, though, someone innocent might end up arrested again.

Mr and Mrs Lynch moved aside to allow us to enter the house.

"If you don't mind my asking, was Andrew acting oddly before his death?" I asked them.

"Very," said Mr Lynch. "He spent most of his time in his room, refusing to speak to anyone. Skipping meals, saying he didn't feel like going to school. That's what he did the morning he—disappeared."

"And was he spending a lot of time in the library?" asked Estelle.

"Yes," said his mother. "He was in there all the time—he

said it was for school, but a few weeks ago, he started going there in the evenings, too."

A few weeks ago—that was around the time Andrew had signed up to the Aspiring Vampires Society.

"We'll get the book from his room," said Estelle.

"Second door on the right," said Mrs Lynch, indicating the staircase to our left.

Estelle and I made our way to the first floor. The door to Andrew's room was closed, but it opened when Estelle pushed it. The room inside appeared typical of a teenage boy —a mess. Clothes everywhere, books on the floor and everything doused in the smell of body spray. Not like a vampire's lair, then. I moved through the room, careful to avoid knocking anything over, and scanned every stack of books in the room in search of the vampire guidebook.

Estelle lifted a pile of textbooks. "Ah, there it is."

The Novice's Guide to Vampirism was a slim volume with illustrations. I picked it up and scanned the notepad underneath the books, but it appeared to contain only blank pages. If he'd been taking notes on how to turn into a vampire, the textbook would tell him everything he needed to know anyway. I looked around the room for possible hiding places and spotted a red glint out of the corner of my eye.

"What are you doing?" Estelle whispered as I pushed a row of books aside on the shelf.

Behind was a row of glass bottles, filled with red liquid. "Somehow, I don't think that's ketchup."

All the bottles were sealed, so I couldn't tell if any had been used, but the sight made nausea creep through me. I moved the books back into place.

"Are you going to tell them?" Estelle whispered.

I shook my head. Considering the bite marks, his parents might have already guessed. For all we knew, he'd acquired the bottles in advance to prepare for his inevitable transformation and had never used them, but either way, telling Andrew's parents wouldn't change the fact that he'd died.

I led the way back downstairs, where Mr and Mrs Lynch waited in the hall. Their gazes passed over the *Novice's Guide to Vampirism*, and Mrs Lynch's face momentarily tightened with fear.

"Have you heard the rumours?" I asked them.

Mr Lynch's mouth hardened. "Vampires? Our son wasn't a vampire. It's disgusting how those rumours get started."

Maybe it's more than a rumour. The words were on the tip of my tongue, but Estelle got there first.

"There were bite marks—"

"Not a vampire," he repeated, his voice firm. "Thank you for returning his cloak."

Estelle nodded. "Sorry for your loss."

There was nothing more to say. Opening the door, I tucked the book into my pocket, leaving the grieving parents behind.

"He's in denial," Estelle muttered when the door closed behind us. "Poor guy."

"No kidding." Andrew had acquired the bottles of blood from somewhere, but unless his parents searched his room, they wouldn't know they were there. Did they count as evidence? Maybe I should have told Mr and Mrs Lynch, but it wouldn't have done us any good.

"Those bottles looked unopened," Estelle added, opening the front gate. "Didn't they?"

"I couldn't tell. Maybe he never had the chance to use them."

Or he hadn't been a vampire for long. Being moody and withdrawn and wanting to go out at night didn't prove anything. I mean, it described most teenage boys I'd met. Add to the fact that the society members had made it their life's mission to emulate the vampires, we needed more proof before making accusations.

"Do you think Cameron was right?" Estelle asked after a moment. "If Andrew argued with Nick before his death, maybe he *was* involved."

"Maybe." Nick wasn't a vampire, so he couldn't have bitten Andrew. But that didn't make him innocent. Perhaps he'd been jealous of Andrew for going ahead with the transformation and attacked him in a fit of rage. But that was pure conjecture.

Like it or not, it did look like Andrew had taken his vampire obsession further than the Aspiring Vampires Society had intended. Which brought me back to Nick—and whatever Jet had overheard him discussing with the others today.

The sooner we learnt to communicate, the sooner I'd be able to find out what Nick was hiding.

———

By the time Estelle and I got back to the library, it was almost closing time. For the last part of the shift, I took over the front desk, reading the *Novice's Guide to Vampirism* while keeping an eye on the door. Unlike my old boss, Aunt Adelaide didn't mind me reading on the job when it was quiet, which was a bonus. I read my way through the chapter titled *Signs that Someone Close to You Might Be a Vampire*. 'Hiding blood bottles' wasn't listed, but being moody, withdrawn, and avoiding people were standard signs. Avoiding rivers, too. Maybe I should ask Andrew's classmates whether he'd avoided crossing any rivers lately, but I didn't think there *were* any in town.

I was so engrossed in the book that I didn't notice someone had come in until a raspy voice said, "Vampires?"

I jumped violently. "Dominic, there's no need to scare me like that."

The well-dressed vampire, who happened to be dating my aunt, scanned the textbook over my shoulder. "That's inaccurate. The time between being bitten, consuming a vampire's blood and transforming should be at least three hours longer."

"Three hours?" I said, momentarily forgetting my annoyance at him for scaring me. "If someone turns, how long does it take, then?"

"If there are no complications after they're bitten, maybe twelve hours," he said. "They remain in a coma-like state for a while. That's why they often rise from the dead after being buried. For that reason, all the bodies of the recently dead are searched for bite marks and handed to the vampires to look after before burial."

"Is it that common?" I asked, making a mental note to avoid any of the town's cemeteries if I could help it.

"No," he said, but the mere hint of pointed canines as he grinned made me want to duck out of sight. I wished I'd never asked. "Andrew hasn't risen from the grave, so he's definitely dead."

"So you know about the case." I held up the *Novice's Guide to Vampirism*. "He checked this out of the library before he died. Then he showed up dead with bite marks in his neck. The leader of the vampires claimed not to have ever met him, though. Have you?"

I expected him to say no, so it surprised me when he answered, "Yes, we've met."

"You have?" I put down the textbook. "When was this?"

"In the library last week," said Dominic. "He wanted me to fact-check his history essay, but when I named my price, he fled."

"Ah," I said. "I guess the students probably pester you

pretty often." Dominic worked as a historian—a fitting job for someone who'd lived for hundreds of years. "Did you notice anything, uh, odd about him?"

"Yes, I did," he said. "Normally, when I speak to someone, I get flashes of their thoughts. It's involuntary in most cases, but it's always there. With him, however, I heard nothing."

I blinked. "What, you couldn't read his mind?"

"No, I couldn't," he said. "I assumed I was mistaken at the time, but when I heard about the bite marks found on his body, it makes a little more sense. If he did decide to turn, he was very foolish, and it's not surprising he met an unfortunate end."

"Someone must have turned him, though," I said. "Right? He can't have done it by himself. And your leader said she'd never met him. Nor did any of the vampire students at the academy."

"I wouldn't know," he said. "So you met Evangeline? What did you think of her?"

"She's… intimidating," I admitted. "Now I appreciate your restraint about not repeating every one of my thoughts back at me."

He grinned, showing another hint of fangs. "She does that to the rest of us, too."

"I thought vampires couldn't read other vampires' minds."

"There are… degrees of ability, you might say," he said. "Those with stronger abilities tend to be elected as leaders. She's lost none of her strength, considering she's over a thousand years old, and she'll know if there are any rogues in town."

"Do you think a rogue bit him, then?"

"Either that or someone is lying." This time when his fangs showed, it looked like a threat. My insides fluttered uneasily.

Who was lying? Andrew couldn't be—he was dead,

vampire or not. But his soul had disappeared. How was that possible?

"Do you think vampires have souls, Aurora?" he asked.

"Can't you read it from my mind?" I responded.

"You seem undecided on the subject."

I shrugged. "I don't know enough about souls to comment. Xavier said he'd never been left in charge of a vampire's soul before..."

"Because Reapers deal with mortal souls. Vampire souls are immortal. We *can* still die, but any knowledge of the matter is closely guarded. Your friend will be sworn to secrecy if he knows."

"But he *doesn't* know how Andrew's soul vanished," I said. "If he was a vampire, though, how can he have drowned? Unless... you can't cross running water, right?"

"No, we cannot, but it's not possible for a vampire to drown," he said, the corners of his mouth turning down. "There are very few ways of killing us. I don't doubt the police have ruled out the major ones after they examined the body."

"He wasn't stabbed or anything, right?" I said. "So how's it possible?"

"Now that is a question I'd like to know the answer to," he said. "If only this remarkable library of yours could provide the answer. It's been an honour speaking to you, Aurora."

He turned his back and was gone, the door lightly closing behind him. *Vampires*. I'd thought he'd come here to speak to my aunt, not me. Compared to Evangeline, Dominic was easy to talk to, but this was the longest conversation I'd ever had with a vampire and he still hadn't given me any real answers. Nor any reason *not* to fear his fellow vampires. Why Nick and the others admired them, knowing what real vampires were like, was a mystery wrapped in an enigma.

Andrew had been bitten, that much was clear, but without

85

their mind-reading advantage, it was beyond me to figure out the culprit. Nobody would know how to kill a vampire better than another vampire, but even Dominic wouldn't want me knowing the vampires' deepest secrets. Besides, it might not have been the same person who killed him.

Hang on—had Dominic seen the forbidden room when he'd looked into my thoughts? Was that what he'd meant when he'd implied the library might be able to give me answers? I'd rather not repeat that particular experience, but if I asked the right question, it might be the only way to find out the vampires' secrets without risking my neck.

"Rory?" Aunt Adelaide approached the desk from behind. "We're closing in five minutes."

"Ah, lost track of time." I closed the textbook. "I got this back from Andrew's parents earlier."

"Oh, Estelle told me," she said. "Such a shame. It seemed like that young man fell in with the wrong crowd."

"What, the vampires?" She didn't know about the secret society, right?

"I heard he joined a foolish group of students who wanted to turn themselves into vampires," she said. "The police are investigating them."

"What, they are?" I said, disarmed. "So—the kid who leads the group is in custody?"

"I've been in the library all day, dear, I wouldn't know," said Aunt Adelaide. "Anyway, it's unbecoming to gossip about the dead."

"If he was murdered, though? Dominic thinks he *was* a vampire, and that means he can't have drowned."

"Is that so?" she said. "Rory, I think you have enough on your plate without interfering with an ongoing investigation."

"Sorry," I said. "Dominic showed up earlier and told me

he couldn't read Andrew's mind, so of course I had to wonder..."

And now the wannabe-vampires were in custody? That meant the police might guess Nick was responsible. But what if he wasn't? If the group had only been a cover, and he had contact with an actual vampire? Someone had helped him transform.

"Leave it to the experts, dear," said Aunt Adelaide. "Have you read the first chapter from your familiar textbook?"

"I have," I said. "I can get Jet to fly to me. That's no problem."

"Excellent." She beamed. "As for your theory classes, you're progressing nicely despite my sister's attempts to derail you. And I assume you've been using your Biblio-Witch Inventory to help you locate books for visitors?"

"I have, but I actually have a question about my biblio-witch magic," I said. "If I wanted to use a spell but not make it permanent, how would I do that? I know whenever I tap the word 'fly', I start flying, but it doesn't last. Would it be the same with any other word I wrote?"

"It depends," she said. "Almost no spell is permanent, but it depends on the strength of the caster, and on whether you write the word in your Biblio-Witch Inventory. Words you use from the Inventory will always be more powerful than ones you haven't used before."

"Oh, of course," I said. When I'd been attacked by vampires who'd started a fire, I'd stopped the flames by writing the word *stop* on a piece of paper when I hadn't even known I was a witch yet. I could still use biblio-witch magic by writing on any nearby piece of paper and most spells would work—they just wouldn't be as strong as if I used one of the spells I'd mastered and written in my Biblio-Witch Inventory.

"Put those books away, dear, and then you can take the evening off," Aunt Adelaide said. "You deserve it."

"Sure." I yawned, closing the textbook. As my aunt walked away, Jet fluttered down and landed on my textbook.

"Did you hear anything from the guy I told you to eavesdrop on?" I asked, lowering my voice. "Nick? The kid wearing the black wig and the cape?"

He cawed and flapped his wings. I assumed that meant yes.

"I suppose he's not happy if they've decided to close down his little secret society," I added. "Or if they arrested him. Did he seem worried when he left earlier?"

Jet gave another caw. Did that mean yes or no?

"Okay," I said. "We're going to try an experiment. Apparently, I can use biblio-witch magic to create a spell so I can understand every word you say. It's not permanent, but I wanted to try it out."

The crow jumped onto the book enthusiastically.

"What, you want me to do it now? I don't know…" I picked up the nearest pen, hesitating. It might not even work. Not every word I wrote turned into magic. It needed that extra *something,* the spark that made biblio-witch magic what it was. Without my proper biblio-witch pen, it might not be strong enough, but I didn't want to try something too strong without practising first.

I pressed the nib of the pen to the page and wrote the word, *speak,* focusing on the crow. I kept the image in my head as firmly as possible, feeling for the spark of magic.

It came. Ink rushed out of my pen, light bloomed around the word, and Jet flapped his wings, fluttering around my head.

"It's an honour to finally be able to speak with you!" said Jet in a squeaky voice.

"Oh!" I dropped the pen. "It worked?"

"Yes, it did!" he squeaked. "I've had so much I wanted to tell you, Mistress."

Mistress? "Uh, do you have to call me that?"

"What would you prefer me to call you?" he asked.

"Just Rory," I said. "Or... er, partner?"

"I like that!" he said. "Partner."

I hadn't been prepared for the spell to work on the first attempt. "I guess you probably know what I wanted to ask you earlier... what did you overhear when you eavesdropped on Nick and his friends?"

He flew around my head with a caw of excitement. "I can finally talk to you, partner! I saw the boy talking to a girl with red hair."

"And what did they say?"

"Many things. Did you know Carla is dating Alice? And it was Ferris who turned Lockwood's toad into a snake?"

"Interesting, but I don't need all the academy students' gossip," I said. "I meant about the murder. Did they mention Andrew Lynch at all?"

"No."

"But you said... you said you heard something useful." Oh, no. I'd misread him, apparently.

"What in the name of the goddess have you done this time?" Cass walked out from the reference section, staring at the crow. "Are you talking to him?"

"I used a communication spell," I said. "I didn't expect it to be that strong."

"What?" She snorted. "You have magic coming out of your ears. Of course it was powerful. Idiot."

"Excuse me? You've been telling me I'm an incompetent excuse for a witch ever since I showed up here."

"And you believed me?" She rolled her eyes. "Whatever. Have fun with your crow."

"You are *not* incompetent!" the crow squeaked.

"I know that now," I said, irate. "Okay, fine, I might need to work on my self-esteem a little, but at least I know you can talk to me now."

"We're going to have so much fun!"

I winced as he squeaked right in my ear. "Yeah, great. Tell you what, can you go and fetch Aunt Adelaide? I should have asked her before doing the spell... I didn't think it would work that fast."

"Didn't you want me to spy on that vampire?" he asked.

"Nick isn't a vampire," I said. "But—all right. You fly around the town at night, don't you? Can you fly outside and tell me if you hear anything weird from any of the people in town? Anything related to Andrew's murder?"

"Done!" He flew out the doors, leaving a gust of wind in his wake.

I think I might have made a mistake.

8

E arly the following morning, a voice squeaked in my ear, "Rise and shine!"

"Ow!" I sat up, rubbing my ears. "Please, not so loud."

"Rise and shine," said Sylvester, in imitation of the crow.

"Shoo." I flapped a hand at them. "Behave."

"But I have news!" said Jet.

"I have news!" echoed Sylvester.

"Watch it." I grabbed for the pen and paper I kept on my bedside table. "According to Cass, I have magic pouring out of my ears. You'd better hope I don't try anything on you next, Sylvester."

"You would never."

I pressed the pen to the page, too half-asleep to think of anything more than a cheap bluff. "Try me."

The owl flew out of the room with a shriek. I sighed and put down the paper. "Do I have a lesson to go to?"

"I know not, partner, but you asked me to spy on the townspeople and I did. William is cheating on his fiancée,

Greg the goblin is stealing from the till at the Black Dog pub…"

"But are either of those things connected to the murder?" I asked.

"No, but Tansy is planning on leaving her husband for a troll, Rebecca thinks Wilhelmina looks like a toad in her new dress…"

Suppressing a groan, I went into the bathroom to shower, leaving the squeaking crow outside the door. He was still mid-monologue by the time I came out of the shower, fully dressed. Apparently, he'd stayed out the entire night gathering gossip from everyone he could find in the town. *Note to self: next time, give him more specific instructions.*

I grabbed my bag, left the room and tripped headfirst down a water slide.

Water filled my mouth, making me choke. My hands flailed, grabbing at the edges, but I was moving too fast to stop. My bag slid ahead of me, crashing into a shallow pool of water, and seconds later, I joined it.

Coughing, I spat out a mouthful of water. "Really, Cass? Now you're wrecking library property?"

The contents of my bag, books included, lay scattered around me—including the *Novice's Guide to Vampirism*, which I'd stayed up late reading. I staggered to my feet, my knees throbbing where I'd landed on them.

"Partner!" said Jet, flying above my head. "Need my help?"

"Yes, I'd like you to find Cass and make her regret this." I shoved a handful of wet hair out of my face and set about picking up my ruined textbooks. Aunt Adelaide had had no trouble restoring the library to its previous condition after the kelpie had rampaged around the ground floor, so if I could make a bird talk, it should be no trouble for me to dry my textbooks.

I picked up the notebook and pen and wrote the word

dry. Immediately, the water vanished from the floor, me, and the books. Even the shallow pool on the floor disappeared. I turned over the notebook. Every page was as dry as it'd been before the water slide incident. The textbooks were in the same condition, without so much as a wrinkle in their pages. Smiling, I opened my Biblio-Witch Inventory to record the new spell.

Aunt Candace's disgruntled voice came from upstairs, "There's no water coming out of the shower!"

Oh, no.

———

Maybe Cass's comment about my magic wasn't inaccurate after all. Not only was the shower not working, the taps weren't, either. Aunt Candace refused to come down without her usual pot of coffee, and while I would have hoped Cass would be grateful that I'd unintentionally got rid of the flood on the third floor, she didn't materialise either. That left it up to Estelle and me to run the place while Aunt Adelaide fixed the damage.

By the end of the morning, I was ready to bury myself in the earth and fake a vampire death myself to get a moment's peace. Jet followed me everywhere I went, telling me any gossip he overheard, and judging by the patrons' confusion at seeing me talking to a bird, I was the only person who could understand him. At this point, I knew everything I didn't want to know about the citizens of Ivory Beach *except* for the people I'd actually wanted him to spy on.

"Can you please go to the jail and see if Nick is still there?" I asked him. "And the other academy students? If they aren't, can you find them and then tell me where they are?"

"Of course I will!" he squeaked, and he flew off.

93

I put my head down on the open record book and groaned.

"What's up, Rory?" Estelle walked over with an armful of textbooks.

I lifted my head. "I messed up. My familiar has turned into the town's newest gossip, but I still don't know who killed Andrew."

"Oh," she said. "You'd think he'd have picked up on something useful, considering he's been flying around eavesdropping on people all day."

"You would think so, but he doesn't know the difference between regular gossip and evidence. All I wanted to know was whether those students are still in jail."

"Nobody's in jail," she said. "None of the students, anyway."

I straightened upright. "How'd you know?"

"Alice told me," said Estelle. "She heard a bunch of students were released from questioning after a lengthy discussion of Andrew's death. Obviously, she doesn't know all the details, about the Aspiring Vampires Society or anything."

"I hope the police do," I said. "I didn't realise they let Nick and the others go. Maybe he isn't the killer. In fairness, I don't see how he can be. There weren't any injuries on Andrew's body other than the bite marks."

Which would suggest he'd drowned, except vampires couldn't, right? We were still missing something.

"Not that I know of," she said. "My mum doesn't want us involved with the vampires. I mean, except Dominic."

"I guess I didn't help with that," I said. "Since I brought three rogues on our tail."

The three vampires who wanted Dad's journal were the only rogues I knew, and maybe it was a sort of misplaced responsibility about that that made me determined to figure out who was responsible for biting Andrew. That, and I was getting concerned that I hadn't heard from Xavier in a while. He'd said he didn't have a phone, but I wished there was an easier way to contact him. I didn't even know where he lived.

The door opened. Jet flew in and landed on the desk in front of me.

"Oh, hey," I said to him. "Sorry, I should have asked if the police released Nick and his friends before sending you out there. Never mind."

"But I thought you would want to know, partner, that they planned on robbing the vampires tonight! A dastardly scheme."

"Who said what now?" I blinked. "I asked you to spy on the Aspiring Vampires…"

"And I did!" he squeaked. "They said they planned to break into the vampires' headquarters tonight. They met on the pier to discuss their foolhardy plan."

"Wait, hold on." I looked at Estelle, whose mouth had parted in disbelief. "You understood that?"

"I—yes. Did you mean for all of us to be able to understand him?"

"No. The other patrons can't." How had I messed up the spell so badly?

"Maybe it's just our family, like Sylvester," she said. "Never mind that—did he say they were going to steal from the vampires?"

I turned back to Jet. "The wannabe-vampires have decided to rob Evangeline? Do they have a death wish?"

He flapped his wings. "Yes, they are. Tonight."

Estelle frowned. "Should we call the police?"

"Would Edwin listen if it hasn't actually happened yet?" I looked around, not seeing any students present. The Aspiring Vampires must have picked out a new meeting point—on the pier, apparently. "They can't have met Evangeline, then. Nobody in their right mind would tick her off."

"They were overconfident enough to pretend to be vampires before," Estelle pointed out. "You're right about Edwin, though. Should we warn the vampires about the impending robbery?"

"That wouldn't go over well. The Aspiring Vampires might have too much confidence, but I'm not sure they know just how dangerous the real vampires are."

Though it was starting to look as though Andrew had been one… for a short time, at least.

"I'll ask Aunt Candace if she can talk to Dominic," Estelle said. "I think she'll have stopped sulking about her coffee by now."

"I hope so." I still hadn't the faintest idea how I'd made all the water in the entire library disappear with a single word.

Estelle walked away, while I remained at the desk, debating. Telling Dominic to warn the vampires might be a wise idea, but if the fake vampires were as incompetent at burglary as they were at secret meetings, then they'd likely get caught straight away. Evangeline didn't seem like the type of person who let thieves go unpunished, and it might be less traumatic if we stopped them before they set foot in the vampires' place.

The sound of a scribbling pen reached my ears, and Aunt Candace stepped out from behind a nearby shelf.

"Don't let me interrupt," she said.

"Didn't you hear Estelle just went looking for you?"

With a shrug, she walked towards me. "I have to congratulate you on your display of biblio-witchery. I don't think even Adelaide could have put a permanent communication spell on her familiar barely two weeks into her magical training."

"Uh, thanks," I said. "But it's not permanent. Is it?" *Please say it isn't.*

"I wouldn't know, dear. I wasn't the one who cast the spell." She grinned. "Please, go on talking to your crow. I could use the material for my next project."

"Trust me, if you had to listen to the town's gossip all day, you'd get bored eventually, too," I muttered.

"You don't want to listen to me?" squeaked Jet.

"That's not what I meant," I said hastily. "I... I just like the quiet. That's why I work in a library."

He shuffled his wings, his gaze downcast. "I understand, partner."

"Wait—"

But he took off in a flutter of wings and was gone.

"I take it he didn't like your honesty?" said Aunt Candace, with far too much smugness. "I have good news, though—the Reaper is here."

"Wait, he is?"

I looked up in time to see Xavier walk in. Aunt Candace stepped back behind the nearest shelf, no doubt with her pen and notebook ready and waiting.

"Hey," I said to Xavier. "You won't believe the day I'm having."

"I can believe it," he said, not looking like his usual cheery self at all. "My boss is throwing a temper tantrum."

"Oh, sorry," I said. "I guess my drama sounds tame in comparison. Aunt Candace, stop eavesdropping."

She poked her head from behind the shelf. "I'm in a creative drought and I have a deadline!"

I shook my head. "It's lunchtime. I'm going to walk to Zee's bakery and get a muffin. Xavier, do you want to come?"

"Sure," he said. "I needed to talk to you anyway."

"Me too." Ignoring Aunt Candace huff at being left behind the desk, I grabbed my bag and hurried outside.

I hadn't lied—I did want one of Zee's amazing muffins after the morning I'd had. I gave Xavier a rundown of my latest mishaps as we walked out of the bakery laden with a bag of delicious muffins and cakes. Maybe I'd gone a little overboard, but I might be able to use them to bribe Jet back so I could apologise to him.

"And I thought I was having a bad day," he said, when I'd finished.

"I'd take Jet over the Grim Reaper." I took a bite of delicious berry-flavoured muffin. "But I feel bad for making him fly off. I don't know where he went."

"He'll come back," said Xavier. "Want to walk to the seafront?"

"Sure. I need to decide who to report the Aspiring Vampires to." The police might pre-emptively arrest them… or they might not believe me. The vampires, on the other hand, might do something scarier and more scarring. The wannabe-vampires struck me as kids playing dress-up, for the most part, and their parents wouldn't want them to end up as vampire snacks. That said, they were still plotting to commit a crime.

"Maybe we should find the kids and talk to them first," Xavier said.

"That'd be the obvious solution, except they're at school right now," I said. "They'll probably come to the library afterwards, but given that their little club got shut down, they might have picked an alternative meeting place. Jet overheard them talking on the pier earlier."

"The pier?" He frowned. "Odd place to meet."

I thought of Andrew's body, tangled in the shallows. Maybe it wasn't the first time they'd been there. "The police let them off the hook before, but I'm having a hard time figuring out how a kid who couldn't even keep his balance on a desk managed to kill a vampire."

"You think Andrew was definitely a vampire, then?"

"He had bottles of blood in his room and bite marks in his neck," I said. "And blood on his cloak, too. Otherwise, I'd have to ask his classmates if he's been avoiding running water and running around at night. Kinda tricky when he and his friends spent weeks pretending to be real-life vampires."

"Just a little," said Xavier, and I detected some of my own frustration in his tone. "The police didn't mention finding any more marks on his body, and as for his missing soul..."

"No more clues?" I asked.

"Unfortunately not. Hence my boss's temper. Souls don't typically go missing on my watch."

"No..." I was still sure it must be linked to Andrew's temporary vampire status, but even the library's question room might not hold all the vampires' and Reapers' deepest secrets. "I wouldn't think vampires would have good reason to murder a teenager either. Even one who was impersonating them."

"No, there's something odd there," he said. "I think we should talk to the police first."

It seemed the best decision, short of going directly to the vampires and finding ourselves on the receiving end of Evangeline's wrath. I doubted Edwin would know how Andrew's soul had disappeared without the Reaper showing up, but we could at least stop the Aspiring Vampires from taking an unnecessary risk.

I finished eating my muffin and went with Xavier into the police station. A female elf wearing blue staffed the front desk and looked at both of us in obvious recognition.

"You again?" she said. "Edwin, it's the Reaper and his friend."

"She's called Rory," said Xavier.

Edwin came out of a side office and gave us both a long-suffering look. "Please tell me you're not here for an update on the murder. I'm aware of your situation, Reaper, but there's been no change since your last visit this morning."

"We're here to report a different crime," he said.

"Oh?" Edwin looked between us. "Do tell."

"Well, it hasn't actually happened yet," I hastened to add. "The students from the academy who you arrested earlier—some of them, anyway—are planning on stealing from the vampires tonight."

His brow furrowed. "Which students, precisely? We can't arrest people for a crime they haven't committed yet without any evidence."

"Nick is one of them," I said. "The kid you arrested earlier. But I'm not sure if anyone else is involved."

"And how exactly did you become aware of this robbery, pray tell?" Both he and the receptionist wore identical sceptical expressions.

"My familiar overheard them talking," I said. "He told me their plan."

Edwin arched a brow. "And can your familiar come here and back you up?"

"I can call him, but uh, I'm the only person who can understand him." A flush heated my neck under their expectant stares. "Jet?"

Unsurprisingly, he didn't respond.

"I think that only works in the library, right?" Xavier supplied.

"If you find your familiar, then you're welcome to bring him here to give evidence," said Edwin, in tones that suggested he was exercising great patience. "In the meantime, I have a murder to investigate."

"But—" He didn't believe me, that much was obvious. "I'm sure Nick and his friends are connected to Andrew's murder."

"All of the students I questioned pleaded innocence and had alibis. They were at the library when Andrew died."

"Wait, they were?" I said.

"Don't you work there?" He shook his head. "Ask your family, if it concerns you. Good day."

Great. I doubted even Aunt Adelaide had taken stock of every single student who'd entered the library that day. I remembered seeing both Nick and the red-haired girl there when I'd come back after finding the body, but Andrew's body might have been in the sea for a while when he'd been found.

"I wasn't morbid in the slightest before I came to live here," I said to Xavier when we left. "Now I'm seeing murderers everywhere."

"Maybe it's because you're in the company of a guy with a scythe strapped to his back," he said.

"Good point." I sometimes forgot he was carrying the scythe at all. It blended into the background, a part of him like his blond curls and aquamarine eyes.

"Shame about Edwin, though," he added. "I think your aunt traumatised him during her brief imprisonment."

"Yeah, that's the impression I'm getting." I sighed. "I shouldn't have gone to report the crime without more evidence than Jet's word, either. Or caused him to fly off."

"I'm sure he'll be back. He's your familiar."

"Sorry, I made it all about me," I said. "You have to deal with the Grim Reaper. That's worse."

"It's not the first time it's happened," said Xavier. "Whenever anything goes wrong, he thinks someone's out to get him. He made me check every one of his scythes was in the exact right place in the storeroom this morning. It took hours, and then he threw a fit because his best scythe was slightly out of position."

"Ouch," I said. "Pity you can't hide in the library until he calms down."

"That was the plan," he said.

"Sorry I dragged you to the police station instead."

"I don't mind, Rory," he said. "You're the one I wanted to see, anyway."

A flush crept up my chest to my neck. Had he actually meant that like I thought? Surely not. I enjoyed spending time with him, too, but his boss was already angry enough without his apprentice disobeying the rules and dating a witch.

"You should get a mobile phone," I found myself saying. "Join the twenty-first century."

"Believe me, I want to," he said. "It'd be nice to check in with you tonight."

"What—you want to intercept the Aspiring Vampires?" *Or is he asking me out?* If he was, I'd probably just blown my chances, but he nodded.

"Perhaps we should," he said. "Before their robbery gets underway. It'll be a lot safer for everyone involved."

"If the Grim Reaper has an issue with it, I can go alone."

"He won't have an issue. If anything, he'd encourage me," he said. "I'm more concerned about you."

My heart missed a beat. "I live in a magical library which regularly thinks it's funny to tip me headfirst down a water slide first thing in the morning. I don't go out looking to take risks, they just sort of... happen."

Xavier's pace slowed as we drew closer to the library. "I thought Cass had stopped pranking you."

"Nope, we're now in a passive-aggressive argument over the kelpie situation."

"She's still mad about that?" He frowned at the library's magnificent facade. "I'll go out with you tonight to check up on the vampires, anyway."

"It's a date." Wait. What did I just say?

"Sure." He grinned, then turned and walked away.

I stared after him for a moment, then fled into the library. Had some bolder person momentarily taken over my body? Firstly, I didn't flirt with people on a regular basis. Secondly, the Reaper was the last person I should be making those kinds of jokes with.

"Hey, Rory." Estelle waved at me from the desk. "You okay? You look kinda spaced out."

"Oh, I'm fine," I said. "Did you find Aunt Candace?"

"She and Dominic are in a fight, apparently."

Huh? Then why was he in the library? "The police weren't much help either. I'd need to take Jet with me to back up my word and nobody but me can understand him."

"Oh," she said. "They didn't believe you? Seriously?"

"I wish they had," I said. "Now the only option is for Xavier and me to find the Aspiring Vampires before the robbery and talk them out of it."

Her brows shot up. "Rory, that's…"

"Risky? Xavier already said that."

"He did?" She tilted her head on one side. "You know, you look a little flustered. Just what were you and Xavier doing? More than going to the police station, right?"

"No," I said firmly. "No, there's nothing going on."

I didn't *think* there was. But thanks to my ill-advised flirting with him, I'd moved into entirely new territory. What was I thinking? I didn't even know the guy's surname.

"I don't see why not." Estelle grinned at me. "You deserve a bit of fun."

"We're dealing with vampires, Estelle. And wannabe-vampires who might also be scheming murderers."

Her grin disappeared. "Do you really think he did it? Nick?"

"I have no idea," I admitted. "He has a motive, but unless

he had help, I don't know how he could have killed Andrew if he was a vampire, let alone made his soul disappear. Still, he's planning a robbery. Maybe it's not his first crime."

"Oh, there you two are," said Aunt Adelaide from behind the desk. "Have you seen your sister, Estelle? I haven't been able to find her all day."

"Wait, where is Cass?" Estelle scanned the lobby, her brow wrinkling.

"Has anyone seen her this afternoon?" asked Aunt Adelaide. "I assumed she was cleaning up the third floor, but she's not there."

"The flood disappeared," I reminded her. "When you undid my spell on the water slide. Did she go out?"

Wait...

"No," said Aunt Adelaide. "She's usually hanging around the third floor or in her room but I checked both and there's no sign of her."

I clapped a hand to my mouth. "Oh, no. I told Jet to play a prank on her earlier, because she made the library tip me down a water slide."

"You did what?" Aunt Adelaide sighed. "Really, Rory, I thought you had more sense. Would you be able to find her?"

"Uh…" *What have I done?* "I'll find her."

"Estelle, I need you down here," said Aunt Adelaide. "Three books are missing from section C23 again."

"Ah." She shot me an apologetic look. "Will you be okay?"

"Sure, I've been up to the third floor dozens of times when I was helping her with Swift," I said. "Maybe she's with the animals and lost track of time."

I hope. Cass might be a menace, but she was still my cousin. I should have given Jet a more specific command, or just not risen to the bait. What if he'd done something irreversible to her?

I ran for the stairs and barely stopped to breathe until I'd reached the third floor. There, I made directly for the rooms containing the living books and those which required special handling. Darting into the short corridor, I pushed at the door to the room where Cass had kept the tank containing the kelpie.

The door didn't give. Locked—from the inside, apparently.

"Cass." I pushed on the door, harder, but it didn't open. Then I pulled out my notebook and pen and wrote, *open.*

The door sprang open in an instant, and a clanking noise came from inside the room, followed by a gasp. Then a rumbling growl that raised the small hairs on my arms.

Oh my god.

The source of the growl was a giant crab-like creature with huge pincers. But most crabs didn't have thick fur or a lion-like head. The beast growled again in its sleep, revealing sharp teeth. *What in the world is that?*

Next to the beast was Cass. She sat at a half-crouch, frozen in position. The cage door hung open—my spell must have hit both doors—but the beast's head was inches away. If it woke up, it'd get out.

"I am going to kill you," she mouthed, moving gingerly towards the cage's open door. Slowly, she climbed out. I held my pen and notebook at the ready, prepared to re-lock the door.

Cass crept out of the cage, straightening upright, then gave me a shove. Hard. We both crashed through the open door into the corridor.

"Ow." I stifled a gasp of pain, one eye on the still-open cage. "Cass, let me go."

"I should lock you up in return," she hissed in my ear.

"Wait, hold on." I scrambled to my feet. "I'm sorry."

"You set that bird on me!" she snapped.

"I didn't know he was going to lock you in the cage," I

said, wondering how in the world he'd managed to lock her into a room when he wasn't much bigger than my palm. "Sorry."

A growl came from behind the door. Uh-oh.

"Good luck," she snarled over her shoulder, stalking away.

Another growl, louder. I grabbed my notebook and pen where they'd fallen to the floor. "Cass, wait. How do I lock the door?"

Not only was it unlocked, there didn't seem to be a lock on the outside at all. And on the other side was the crab-lion thing.

Oh, no.

The door nudged open and a giant pincer came out. I stabbed the page with my pen, scrawling the word *fly.*

The crab-lion flew back into the air with a roar. A tremendous rustling noise came from behind me, and I spun around in horror as all the books on the shelves took flight at the same time. Rustling sounded, the clamour of a thousand books escaping into the air...

"Stop!" I yelled frantically. The door was wide open, showing me the crab-lion flailing around in mid-air, but I hadn't the faintest idea how to undo the spell without setting it loose again.

"What've you done this time?" Sylvester said from behind me. "You brought in a manticore?"

"No, I didn't," I protested. "Help me undo this spell."

"I'm going to pretend you said 'please'," Sylvester said, flapping his wings.

There came a rushing sound, and the manticore landed on the floor in front of the cage. Before it could move, the door closed, and there was the click of a lock.

I turned slowly around, already knowing I'd find all the books back on the shelves where they belonged.

"Since when did you have magic?" I looked at Sylvester in

disbelief. There were thousands of books on this floor alone. *How did he do that?*

"Just because I don't waste mine on trivial nonsense, doesn't mean I have no talents," he said.

The manticore howled from behind the door, and I backed away. I'd had quite enough close brushes with death for one day.

9

When I left the library with Xavier at nine that night, I figured that unless the night ended with me stuck in the vampires' lair, it couldn't be worse than what I'd experienced this week already.

Cass wasn't speaking to me. Aunt Adelaide seemed ticked off, too, though she understood that Jet had been the one who'd taken my revenge request too far. The crow himself had yet to reappear after his earlier flight. Only Aunt Candace was in a good mood, walking around humming in a manner that suggested everyone's misery was the perfect fuel for her novel.

"Chasing vampires feels like a breath of fresh air," I said to Xavier, shivering in the ocean breeze chilled with December's frost. "Cass will probably have turned my bed into a coffin by the time I get home. Where do the vampires live, anyway? In a crypt?"

"Almost," said Xavier. "There's an old manor house next to the local cemetery. Most of the elder vampires live in there. The younger ones don't, but that's Evangeline's base."

"I should have guessed," I said. "If we were foolish

teenagers plotting to steal from the vampires, where would we meet up first? The pier?"

"Maybe," he said. "I don't think it'll be hard to spot them at night, considering they're too young to go out drinking."

He wasn't wrong. The town didn't have much in the way of nightlife, but most people went to the pubs on the seafront at night if they felt like braving the cold. The streets on the other side of the square were dark and deserted and I found myself glad of Xavier's company. Walking through dark streets at night was less scary with a Reaper at my side.

"Would it kill them to put in more street lamps?" The sea looked like an endless mass of blackness in which anything might be lurking, and the pier resembled a desolate location from a horror movie.

"Nah, that'd kill the atmosphere," he said. "I agree, it's a bit dark and creepy."

"Coming from the angel of death."

He chuckled and strode ahead, his steps confident. We found nobody on the pier, however, so Xavier led the way back through the square and down the high street. At night, the windows' bright displays took on sinister undertones. The robe-wearing mannequins in the clothes shops looked unnervingly like shadowy figures waiting to jump us, but Xavier's confident pace didn't slow. A sinister empty street to him was like a sunny beach to normal people. Or to me, a room full of books.

"Almost there," he said.

Sure enough, the outline of the old manor house came into view as we turned left into a side street that sloped uphill. The house was as grand as I'd expected, with arched windows and carved balconies, and had been fenced off— maybe to protect the people who lived in the houses nearby from its vampire inhabitants. What if they were hanging around in the shadows watching us right now?

Don't think about that, Rory. The vampires might be creepy, but they weren't the ones plotting a crime tonight.

"I don't think they're here, Rory," muttered Xavier.

He seemed to be right: nobody else was about. Living or otherwise.

"They might be running late or have lost their burgling equipment or something." Maybe their parents had put their feet down and stopped them. Or they'd come to their senses. The Aspiring Vampires Society had been forced to disband, and they'd narrowly avoided a stint in jail. Committing another crime right away was foolish at best.

"Now, what are you two doing here?" said a soft voice.

I turned around, my body tensing. Evangeline stood outside the gate of the old manor house as though she'd been there all along, watching us with her head tilted on one side.

"Nothing," I said stupidly. "I mean, just enjoying the nice winter night. Going for a stroll."

"Are you?" She raised a perfect eyebrow. "It seems an odd place for a witch like you to take a stroll, with so little light to see by. All these houses belong to creatures of the night. I would have thought the Reaper would have wanted to avoid straying so close to his own territory, too."

His own territory?

"Maybe the Reaper has his reasons," said Xavier. "I assumed you were busy tonight. Not teaching at the academy?"

"That's merely a hobby. New vampires are so... fresh. Are you looking for company?" She smiled widely.

"Very kind of you to offer, Evangeline," said Xavier. "As a matter of fact—"

"You're here to prevent a robbery." She looked squarely at me. "A robbery committed by human teenagers. Interesting. Do you know what I did to the last human to steal from the vampires?"

"No." *I shouldn't have come.* As long as I couldn't shield my thoughts from her, there was no keeping any secrets. "I'm assuming they didn't live to tell the tale?"

"Oh, he lived, all right, but he wished he didn't." She gave another smile. "It's lucky those human teenagers didn't show up, isn't it?"

Her stare bored into me as though she could see right into the depths of my soul. I averted my eyes and took a step back. "Never mind, then," I said. "We'll be going."

"I don't think so," she said softly. "Do you mean to tell me you suspect one of these humans of knowing how to murder a vampire?"

"No."

Evangeline's eyes narrowed and her lips pulled back a fraction, exposing her pointed canines. "Don't lie to me."

I wanted to reply, *don't invade my privacy,* but nothing came out.

"It's just a theory," Xavier put in. "We don't even know if Andrew was really a vampire when he died. Since he had bite marks on his neck, it's possible that whoever killed him did know how to kill a vampire, but he wasn't a very experienced one."

"He had no marks on his body aside from the ones in his neck, I recall," said Evangeline. "Interesting."

"Do—do you know how it might be possible?" I asked.

An inexplicable smile curled her lip, emphasising her fangs. "Nice try, young Aurora."

"I don't know what you—" *Oh.* She thought I was trying to find out how to kill a vampire for my own reasons. Definitely not. I'd happily forget everything I knew about vampires forever if only they left me alone. "I just want to find out who killed Andrew, to help the poor kid's family get some closure."

She moved forwards, and I instinctively stepped back. I

didn't think I'd ever get used to the fast, fluid way vampires moved, as though they were fully aware that every atom of them was different to the rest of us. "Is that your only motive, Aurora? You can't shield your curiosity from me. Your mind is positively brimming with questions. You'd think living in a magical library would have solved at least some of your thirst for knowledge."

"I assumed there were some things you kept to yourself," I said. "Never mind. Forget I asked."

"Evangeline," said Xavier, in a warning tone. "There's no need to frighten her. She's not doing any harm."

Her gaze snapped to him. "Do you presume to give me orders, apprentice? It's unbecoming of a Reaper."

"You're in a position of authority. It's unbecoming to use that position to intimidate Rory," he said.

I wished I had his courage. Then again, he probably couldn't be affected by a vampire bite, so he had nothing to lose by ticking her off.

Evangeline stepped back, just fast enough to show me the distance she'd put between us didn't matter. If she wanted to bite me, I'd have no way of stopping her.

I clenched my shaking hands. "He's right. Intimidating me won't change the facts. And for the record, there *are* some things that aren't in the library. For instance, I'm assuming you know the rogue, Mortimer Vale, has a couple of friends who are after me?"

"Yes, but nobody specified why," she said. "Oh, a journal written in code? Interesting."

Argh. I shouldn't have even thought about it. But she'd probably known about the journal from the instant we'd first locked eyes. Her surprise now was just an act.

"Don't worry, I won't intrude," she said. "I *am* curious to see this journal, but not enough to invade your privacy."

I didn't have to be able to read minds to know that for a

blatant lie. And while the library was protected against intruders, she was the vampires' leader. If she wanted to look at the journal, there was little I could do to stop her.

"It's not that important," I said, my throat dry. "I can't read it. Nobody can. If the code document ever existed, Abe probably threw it out."

Her eyes locked to mine, and I forced my mind back to the day I'd found the journal in the back of the shop, where Abe had been throwing it into the bin. I let the argument play out in my mind as clearly as I remembered it. *Why do you want to keep an old piece of junk like that? It was probably one of Roger's weird projects,* Abe had said. *Nothing important.*

Evangeline tilted her head on one side. *I'm not hiding anything, and I'm not lying,* I thought. Besides, Mortimer Vale had tried to take the journal from me and ended up jailed for it.

She gave a soft laugh as though she'd overheard my last thought before I'd slammed a lid on it. "Interesting. I have to say... your arrival is one of the most intriguing events that's happened in this sleepy town for a long time. Maybe you should stroll this way more often."

"Aren't you bothered about the idea of people stealing from you?" Xavier said, taking a step closer to me. "If you ran into these teenagers, you'd hand them over to the authorities, right? There's no need to take action yourself."

"As you rightly said, Reaper, I *am* the authority," she said. "It's been delightful seeing you."

And in a whisper of a step, she was gone. I stood still for a moment, cursing my heart for hammering like there was a monster after me. Even if it was kind of true.

Xavier's hand touched my shoulder, and I jumped. "Sorry," he whispered. "I guess we tried."

I inched closer to him, feeling a little less cold than before despite the fact that he wasn't much warmer than the freezing air. "You're right. We tried. If they want to steal from the vampires after all this, it's on them."

"You want to go back?" He frowned, lifting his chin. "Hear that?"

Footsteps sounded on the pavement, somewhere ahead on our left. Around the back of the vampires' home.

I raised an eyebrow. "They're late."

Xavier trod lightly alongside the fence. I followed, wishing I had the same talent for making my footsteps go silent. Perks of being a Reaper—or vampire. The distinct sound of feet tapping on the road proved the people sneaking around nearby didn't have that skill, either.

"It's the Reaper!" someone yelled, and three figures wearing cloaks tripped out of the shadows, falling over like skittles.

To no surprise, one of them was Nick. The others were Zach, the boy with the dreadlocks who'd been responsible for the failed invisible ink, and Gail, the red-haired girl who'd dated Andrew before his death.

"What are you doing?" I walked over to them. "Do you have a death wish?"

"What are *you* doing?" said Nick, scrambling to his feet, only to trip over the end of his cloak and face-plant again. He came upright a second time, his nose bleeding. A pair of fake vampire fangs lay on the pavement and he picked them up, his pale face flushing.

"Visiting the vampires' leader," I said. "Should I tell her you were sneaking into their headquarters?"

He winced, his nose continuing to drip blood. "No!"

"Then you admit you were going to steal from them?" Xavier said. "Would you rather speak to the police?"

"I didn't do anything!" Something fell from his pocket and rolled over on the ground and he scrambled to pick it up.

"Give that here," Xavier said. "Is that what it looks like?"

Nick scowled and held the glass container out of reach, but even in the gloom, the glowing red dust caught my eye.

"That's firedust," I said. "What were you going to do, set the vampires' home on fire?"

He looked down. "No. It was just in case we got cornered…"

"You realise that's illegal, don't you?" said Xavier. "Give that here."

He walked towards Nick, who reluctantly handed over the container. I suppressed a shudder at the memory of what that firedust had nearly done to Dad's old shop. Not to mention the library.

"Nick!" shouted a voice. A witch wearing a bright pink dressing gown stormed down the street A matching pointy hat perched on her head, and her glare was trained on Nick.

"I think," Xavier muttered in my ear, "she might be his mother."

The witch strode over to the three abashed-looking teenagers, straightening her pointy hat. "What are you doing? You're bleeding all over your dad's cloak, Nick."

I stifled an unexpected snort, and Nick shot me a furious look as his mother fussed over him. "Really, Nick. You're not still playing those ridiculous games?"

"It's not a game," he mumbled.

"Clearly not, if you're dragging your friends into it as well." She waved her wand, conjured a tissue and handed it to him, where he pressed it to his bleeding nose. "Childish, reckless, and absurd." She paused for breath, her gaze landing on Xavier and me.

"And you are?" she asked. "The Reaper, correct?"

"I'm Xavier." He held out the jar of firedust. "Where did your son get this?"

"Good question." She snatched the container from him,

her gaze travelling to me. "I'll be asking him in detail later. And you are?"

"I'm Aurora Hawthorn. I work at the library."

"Oh, Adelaide's niece. Tell her I said hello."

"Er… sure," I said, slightly nonplussed. She didn't seem to be scared of Xavier at all.

"As for *you*—" she turned to the other two teenagers—"I hope your parents will be as concerned as I am about your childish schemes. The vampires aren't a joke, and they aren't anything to aspire to."

I hoped Evangeline and her fellow vampires weren't listening in. Otherwise, we might get caught in a standoff between a furious mother in a dressing gown and the leader of the vampires.

"Now, come on. All of you. Now." She beckoned with a finger, then marched away. The three teenagers trailed after her without a word.

I turned to Xavier. "And I thought I'd already seen it all."

"The vampires must have heard her," Xavier remarked. "There's no chance they weren't listening in, but I guess they didn't want to get into the middle of their argument."

Nick half-ran over to me. His nose was still bleeding, and it was even more obvious the cloak was too big for him now.

"You!" he yelled at me. "You did this. You got me grounded for a month."

"I stopped you getting yourself in trouble with the vampires," I said. "I'd rather be grounded than the vampires' prisoner."

"I wouldn't have got caught," he insisted.

"They can read your mind, Nick," I said. "The instant you got into their home, the vampires would all know you carried that dust and they'd assume you meant to burn all of them."

Nick's face paled. "They wouldn't. I didn't plan to actually

116

use the firedust on them."

"I doubt that would matter to Evangeline," Xavier said. "Especially given that you were just released from questioning about a murder."

Nick took a step backwards. "I didn't kill Andrew."

"I'm told you argued with Andrew before he died," I said. "Want to tell me about that? Because it sounds like you didn't tell the police everything."

"He started it," he said defensively. "He kept trying to tell me how to run the group. Getting under my feet. Telling me he'd become a vampire first."

"Did he?" I said. "Would that give you a reason to figure out a way to kill a vampire? Because it doesn't look good for you."

His face reddened. "I don't know how to kill a vampire."

"You spend every Monday studying it." *And you were carrying firedust in your pockets.*

"We never got that far," he mumbled. "Because you shut down our society."

"Good job I did, then," I said. "Because you clearly need a lesson in common sense."

"Nick, get over here!" his mother bellowed.

He winced and turned away, stumbling over his dad's cloak as he did so.

"He's lying," I whispered to Xavier. "Why did the police let him go?"

"Because he was in the library when Andrew's body was found."

That proves nothing. He could easily have committed the murder and then left the scene, hiding among the other students. With no witnesses, it was anyone's guess.

"If he *is* the killer, then his mother won't let him out of her sight anytime soon," Xavier added.

"No, I guess not." I looked around the deserted street. "I

can't believe he had that firedust. Where'd he even get that?"

"I bet he stole it," he said. "Killer or not, he's got a future behind bars the way he's going."

"All because he wants to be a vampire." I let my gaze pass over the deceptively quiet house. "You know we're probably being watched, right?"

"Of course we are." He narrowed his eyes at the grand manor house. "They must have chosen not to interfere. I can't say I know why."

He turned his back on the vampires' place and began to walk away. I did likewise, relieved to let the vampires thoroughly out of my sight.

"How far does vampire hearing carry?" I said in a low voice. "Is it safe to say I think Evangeline is a creepy, nosy eavesdropper? She wants to see the journal. I had bloody enough of that from the other three."

"Ah." His mouth pinched. "Tell your aunt and I can guarantee she'll find a way to protect it."

"*I* should be able to protect it," I mumbled, feeling a rush of shame. I might have faced my fears today, but I was way out of my depth. But I knew one thing: Dad wouldn't want any vampires to touch the journal. Even the ones who didn't want to steal it.

"You did great tonight," Xavier said softly. "Nick was scared of you."

"Nick was scared of his mother," I reminded him, but I smiled. "Glad I didn't have to use magic on him. The way things are going today, I'd have made the whole street disappear."

"You can do that?"

"Maybe," I said. "When I tried to clean up a flood, I accidentally disappeared *all* the water in the library and Aunt Candace was in the shower at the time."

He laughed. When he did, his eyes lit up, like I was

looking at a human, not a Reaper. "I wish I'd been there."

"Trust me, you don't," I said. "But—I'm glad I came out tonight. Even though we never proved a crime was committed."

"I think we stopped any future crimes from that particular group, so I vote this evening a success." He moved a little closer to me as we walked, his hand brushing against mine. My heart skipped a beat. Had he done that on purpose?

"Do you have plans tomorrow?" he asked.

Yes. He did do it on purpose. I found myself fervently glad *he* couldn't read my spinning thoughts.

"Avoiding Cass, magic lessons… the usual." My mood dimmed. "I really messed up today. Not only did I drive my familiar away, I told him to get revenge on Cass for pranking me and he locked her in a cage with her own pet manticore. And then I accidentally levitated all the books on the third floor trying to get her out. I should have just waited for Cass to get bored rather than retaliating."

"I doubt that would have stopped her," he said. "It's better to let yourself get angry than bottle it up, or she'll keep pushing your boundaries."

"Hmm." He might have a point. "Now she really has it in for me, and I think Aunt Adelaide's mad at me, too."

"She'll get over it," he said. "That aside, are you enjoying Ivory Beach? I keep meaning to ask you how you're adjusting. I know these things can take a while."

"Honestly, I love it here," I said. "Estelle's a great friend, and my aunts always make things entertaining. I feel like I've been here years, not weeks."

A twinge of guilt hit me. I hadn't seen my former best friend Laney since I'd moved to the library. Laney was my only link to my old life—a life that seemed further away with every day that passed. She'd be proud of me for what I'd achieved so far. I knew that much.

"I'm glad," said Xavier. "I worried Evangeline might have ruined your impression of the magical world."

"No, but I wish I'd done a better job of standing up to her," I said. "I feel like I let her walk all over me."

"Nah, you just have a healthy sense of self-preservation," said Xavier. "Don't forget I can't die."

"No…" But looking at him now, he didn't appear to be anything but alive. His eyes gleamed an impossible shade of aquamarine, and his head tilted closer to mine.

A howling noise struck up, making me jump. "What was that?"

"Werewolves?" He quirked an eyebrow. "We haven't been to that part of town yet…"

"I think vampires are more than enough for one night, thanks." I held a hand to my thumping heart, my gaze picking out the fence bordering a cemetery on our right-hand side. "Not zombies, is it?"

"I hope not, considering I live in there."

"You do?" I peered over the fence, but the night was so dark, and the lights so dim, all I could see were the shadowy outlines of gravestones.

"Not under the ground," he added. "There's a house further up there, which belongs to the Reaper. My boss is still going on at me about his scythes being slightly out of place. Anyone would think he was the one under threat of a robbery. I'll walk you home, anyway."

I stared over the cemetery gate for a moment, his words ringing through my mind. Maybe I was jumping to conclusions, but perhaps… perhaps he had a point.

Though I didn't say a word to Xavier, a chilling certainty began to settle over me.

The killer hadn't stolen from the vampires.

They'd stolen from the Grim Reaper.

10

I might have faced my fears, but the idea of curling up with a book for the rest of the night had never been more appealing. When Xavier waved goodbye on the doorstep, I almost broke and told him what had occurred to me, but without proof, there wasn't anything he could do.

If Nick—assuming he was the killer—had stolen the scythe, why had he returned it? To cover his tracks? Maybe he hadn't meant to kill Andrew, but as Xavier had said, all the signs pointed to another Reaper being responsible for Andrew's missing soul. If someone else had stolen his scythe, maybe it would have the same effect.

But without proof, would the Reaper believe me?

Telling Xavier my suspicions would have to wait. The instant the library door closed behind me, the lights went off.

"Really funny, Cass," I said. The lanterns that usually lit up the library were shrouded in darkness, casting an aura of gloom over the elegant shelves. I'd seen my aunts and cousins have no trouble turning the lights on and off with a snap of the fingers, but Cass knew perfectly well I was miles away from being a master biblio-witch with control over the library itself.

Wishing my notebook and pen glowed in the dark, I fumbled in my pockets. "Turn the lights back on, Cass."

Silence answered. I took a step forward and tripped into nothingness. Choking on a scream, I threw out my arms, then I landed face-first on a soft surface.

Heart hammering, I lay face-down, smelling something distinctly musty. I knew that smell. I'd landed in the vampire's basement. "Really, Cass. You already tried this one."

Granted, last time I'd actually been able to see where I was going. Knowing there was a vampire in an unseen coffin somewhere close by made goose-bumps creep up my arms. I sat up, digging in my pockets for my notebook and pen. Grasping the pen in my hand, I wrote the word, *light.*

Dazzling brightness pierced my sight. I squeezed my eyes shut, then opened them, but the lights were still blazing.

"Turn it off!" yelled a voice from above.

"I don't know how." Oh, no. I'd done it again. What if I'd permanently blinded everyone in the library?

I opened my eyes a fraction and squinted at the word on the page. Light... hang on. I'd once undone a spell by changing the words on a page. What if I could do the same now?

I scrawled through the word *light,* erasing it from view.

At once, the blinding light vanished. I blinked the glare from my eyes, looking around the basement. In the coffin to my right, the vampire was still asleep. Thank heavens for small mercies.

Problem: a real-life, awake vampire was looking down at me from the trapdoor above my head. "Oh, it's you, Dominic."

"You nearly fried me to death," he said in accusing tones.

"Sorry," I said. "I didn't know you were here. Anyway, it was Cass who turned out the lights and caused me to trip down a trapdoor."

I pocketed my notebook and pen and pulled out my Biblio-Witch Inventory, tapping the word *fly.*

"Heads up," I said, as my body left the ground, lurching out of the trapdoor.

Dominic stepped aside with dizzying speed, catching my arm before I went spinning up to the ceiling. My feet hit the ground and my knees buckled. Why did I so easily forget about vampires' super-strength and speed?

"You're welcome," he said, releasing me.

"Ah, thanks," I said, uncomfortable with the way he was scowling. His fangs seemed more prominent than usual, unless I was just jumpy. I stepped away from the trapdoor, but not before he'd set eyes on the room below.

"Who is that vampire?" he asked, peering into the basement.

"He's a friend of my grandma's," I said. "Nobody knows who he is, but he's been asleep in there for a while."

Nobody outside of our family knew about the vampire— known as Albert to my aunts—but it was Cass's fault Dominic had had to come to my rescue. If she got angry at me for sharing the family's secrets, it wasn't my problem this time.

"Your family certainly has no end of surprises." He closed the trapdoor firmly.

"Sorry about the lights," I said. "Cass needs to get some new ideas. That's the second time she's tossed me into the basement."

"I assume it's because she knows about your fear of vampires," he said.

"I'm not afraid," I said, ineffectually. "Not as much as I

used to be, anyway. I've just seen too many vampires tonight not to be a little twitchy."

"You spoke to Evangeline again?" He raised an eyebrow.

"I didn't plan to," I said. "I heard some of the academy kids planned to steal from the vampires tonight, and Xavier and I went to intercept them. Evangeline did her usual trick where she read every thought from my mind, including things I'd have preferred her not to know." Like the journal. Sure, it wasn't much use as long as I couldn't read a word, but that didn't give her the right to poke her nose into my business. The journal was Dad's.

Dominic looked at me, his head tilted on one side. I wondered how many of my thoughts he'd seen. "There *are* ways to shield your thoughts, you know. If you focus on one particular image, it'll stop her from reading your stray thoughts. Keep your chosen image in your mind until the vampire's attention moves away from you."

"Not sure that'll work out for me," I said. "I tend to have a busy mind. And when you tell me not to think about penguins, the first thing I'm going to do is think about penguins."

"Why penguins?" he said. "Any subject would do. I would prefer it if you didn't mention to Evangeline that I told you that."

"I won't, but... I can't promise I won't think about it," I admitted. "I don't have a huge amount of control over what I think about."

"Then I'd suggest you learn it." The corners of his mouth turned down, exposing his prominently pointed canines.

"Hang on," I said. "Didn't you use a fang-shrinking curse?"

"Why?" he said, a touch of defensiveness in his tone. "What does that have to do with anything?"

"Just wondering." I shouldn't have brought it up, but he'd sought out a fang-shrinking curse when he started seeing my aunt... not that I was keen to imagine why, exactly.

"Not anymore," he said. "Your aunt and I broke up."

"Oh," I said. "Sorry. Was it because of me? Or Cass?"

"No, we came to a mutual decision to go our separate ways," he said. "I was on my way out when the lights switched off."

"Sorry to hear that." I was, too. Dominic was a decent guy. "I've had a weird night as well. And Evangeline will probably show up here next to have a look at my dad's journal. Does she know about this... secret group, whoever Mortimer Vale works for?"

"I can't say we've ever discussed it," said Dominic, his voice cold. *Oh. He must be remembering his stint in jail.* I had once suspected him of conspiring with Aunt Candace to steal it, after all. But he was much less scary than Evangeline was. "If it bothers you, I'd suggest you avoid her until you become more adept at shielding your thoughts."

He strode away through the shelves, and the sound of the door closing behind him sounded through the quiet library.

Cass stepped out from behind a shelf a moment later. "He's right, you know. You're in way over your head."

"And you have too much free time on your hands," I responded. "Look, I'm sorry about Jet. And the manticore. I didn't know you'd brought *another* dangerous animal into the library."

She rolled her eyes. "Yeah, right. Admit it, you enjoyed it."

"Don't be absurd," I said. "Why would I spend weeks helping you with your pet kelpie and then try to kill you?"

"He wasn't a pet." She walked away through the dark lobby. Over her shoulder, she added, "And if that's the case, then you're way too soft to handle the vampires. They'll eat you alive."

Maybe she was right, but I doubted Evangeline would

drop her interest in the journal that easily. Dominic's advice might work on a less powerful vampire, but surely their leader would be wise to any trickery. More annoyingly, I'd forgotten to tell Dominic about my suspicions regarding the Reaper's involvement in Andrew's death. He was the one person who might take me seriously for suggesting it. Then again, he'd been in an odd mood after breaking up with my aunt, and I had no proof. I didn't want to provoke the Reaper's wrath without being certain.

You're way too soft to handle the vampires. Maybe I was, but I'd rather be soft than cold and prickly like Cass was. I didn't think she actually did get any enjoyment out of pranking me. She was just looking for an outlet because her one companion had run off and she blamed me for it.

That means I have to figure out how to get Swift back if I want her to forgive me.

———

The following morning, Jet didn't wake me up by chirping at me. Nor did he come when I called him, though I tried several times from different parts of the library. Even Sylvester ignored me while I was running all over the library handling returns. Thanks to the spell I'd used to levitate all the books yesterday, dozens of them had ended up in the wrong sections. *Maybe I should take a break from magic until I get my act together.*

When I carried a stack of history books across the ground floor, I spotted a study group in session in the Reading Corner. The academy's students were here for the morning, and sure enough, Nick sat at a table with his friends. I changed my route to pass behind their group, trying to over-hear their conversation, but Nick saw me first. His eyes narrowed.

I averted my gaze and returned the books to the correct shelves. When I walked past the table, a bottle of ink flew at me, spraying everyone nearby.

"Oops," said Nick. "Sorry."

"Oh, there's the invisible ink," said Zach, his friend. "Bad luck."

"Did you say invisible—" Sure enough, while my coat showed dark stains and so did the carpet, the ink appeared colourless. I pressed a fingertip to the carpet, and it came away damp and smelling slightly of ink, but not stained.

Nick leaned over and grabbed the bottle as it rolled to a stop. "What's it doing in here? This is supposed to be normal ink."

"Did you switch the bottles?" said Zach, with a snicker.

"Keep it down," said Gail.

"Everyone already knows," said Nick, pulling out a wand.

"No magic in the library," I said. I'd hardly raised my voice, but they all froze. I must have sounded more disciplinary than I'd thought.

"I was going to get rid of the ink," said Nick.

"I'll do it." I dug my hand in my pocket, pulled out my notebook and got transparent fingerprints over the pages as I turned them. Wait, maybe I shouldn't use biblio-witch magic to remove the ink from the carpet. Aunt Candace would never forgive me if I made every speck of ink in the library vanish.

"What is going on?" Aunt Adelaide asked from behind me.

"Invisible ink," I explained, indicating the stained carpet. I'd hardly touched it, but somehow the ink had ended up on all my fingers. Not to mention my notebook.

As my aunt waved her wand, making the ink vanish, I flipped my notebook closed, tearing out the page I'd got inky fingerprints all over.

Then I frowned, looking more closely at the page. There

was a word written there that I hadn't noticed before, scrawled in the same transparent font as the ink on my fingers.

Someone had put invisible ink in my book and used it to write the word *'amplify'*. And I'd bet I knew who it was.

Cass, I am going to kill you this time.

I sucked in a deep breath, marched back to the table, and snatched up the invisible ink bottle from in front of a bewildered Nick. "I'm confiscating this."

The students blinked, confused, as I walked away with the ink bottle in hand. Once I was out of their line of sight, I turned to the offending notebook page again and tipped the ink over the word *amplify*, erasing it. That ought to do it.

I checked my notebook to make sure Cass hadn't hidden any more words in invisible ink and hesitated on the page where I'd written the familiar spell. Intentional or not, I didn't want to permanently switch it off. I needed to mend things with Jet first.

"Ah, excuse me? Miss?"

I turned around. Cameron stood behind me, looking abashed.

"Call me Rory," I said. "Did you need my help with something?"

"No, I just wanted to apologise for the ink," he said. "Nick and his friends are trouble-makers."

"I know." Did he know about last night? Maybe. Not being a vampire, it wasn't like he could read my thoughts.

"Yeah, he's supposed to be grounded," said Cameron. "That's what everyone is saying. They say he got caught last night trying to rob the vampires."

His tone didn't make it clear whether he'd heard about me being there or not. It didn't really matter if everyone knew, unless the Reaper was bothered by me and Xavier going for night-time strolls together. I doubted it, though. He had much bigger problems if my hunch about the killer borrowing his scythe were true.

I weighed the odds, then said, "Yeah, I was there, actually."

Cameron's brows rose. "You were?"

Something in his tone rang false. Like he'd known, but he wanted to pretend it was a surprise.

"Yes," I went on. "I heard a rumour that they planned to steal from the vampires and decided to go there to make sure they didn't get into trouble."

"Where'd you hear it?" There was a note of caution in his voice.

"They held their meetings here in the library," I said. "I work here. Why? You're not part of their group, right?"

"No, but I heard some of their ideas." He looked down. "At first, they just wanted to become more like the vampires, but they used to do it from a distance. Now they're stealing from them."

"That's not all they stole, is it?" I was thinking of the fire-dust, but the scythe came to mind.

Cameron paled. "I..."

"Do you know something?" I tried not to sound too harsh. He was just a kid, really.

He swallowed. "Uh. I heard they sneaked into the apothecary. I should have reported them, but I got cold feet." There was a genuine-sounding tremor in his voice.

Time to cut to the chase. "Nick was already questioned by the police. Do *you* think he was the killer?"

"I... don't know," he said. "He's unpredictable. And he's the sort of guy who'd see killing a vampire as a badge of honour. Like stealing from them."

"You should have reported them, you know."

"I did," he mumbled. "I told Nick's mother. Too late, but at least nobody was hurt."

Oh, that's how she knew. "If you see anything in the future,

I'd really appreciate it if you told either me, the police, or someone else in an authority position *before* it happens."

"Okay," he said. "Er, maybe Gail was involved, too. I'm not sure. But they dated and were close friends before that. She's still in Nick's inner circle."

All right, I'll talk to her next. Odd that he'd chosen to confide in me—or maybe it wasn't. From the way the students had acted when I'd told them off, they saw me as an authority figure. I hadn't meant to intimidate the poor kid, but on the other hand, maybe I could use my perceived authority to my advantage.

As Cameron walked away, I followed him into the study area. Aunt Adelaide stood watching the students, including Nick. Gail, however, wasn't there. I turned around and spotted her returning a book to the shelf on my right.

"Hey," I said, walking over to her. "Can I talk to you alone?"

She looked down, biting her lip. "I didn't do anything. I didn't know he was going to throw ink at you."

"I know you didn't," I said. "I just wanted to have a word with you about Andrew."

Her shoulders tensed. "What about him?"

I lowered my voice. "You knew he was actually a vampire, right?"

"I… yeah." She didn't quite meet my eyes, but her posture relaxed.

"And whose idea was last night's scheme?" I asked. "You must have known that stealing from the vampires would go badly."

"Yeah…" She chewed on her lower lip again, her cheeks pink. "I didn't want Nick to get himself killed over a stupid accident. I thought if I went along, he was less likely to run into trouble."

"He's still grounded, right? He's not going to have too many opportunities to go near the vampires' place?"

"Not if his mother has anything to do with it," she said.

Good. I paused, then said, "Were you there when he stole the firedust?"

Her mouth pressed together. "I don't want him to be jailed. He's an idiot, but he... he's just misguided."

"Did you think the same about Andrew?" I asked. "Did he steal, too?"

She looked away. "What does it matter? He's dead."

"And his parents don't know how it happened," I said. "I won't report you if you tell me the truth."

Unless it turns out you were involved with the murders, that is.

"Only from the blood bank," she mumbled.

Of course. I should have known he'd got those bottles of blood from somewhere.

"Whereabouts is the blood bank?" I asked.

"At the hospital, of course," she said, fidgeting. "That's all I know, I swear."

"You can tell me if you remember anything else," I said. "I won't tell your parents. Unless it threatens someone's life, but that goes without saying. I don't have a stake in this. Er, not in a literal or metaphorical sense. I'm just trying to help a friend."

"Me too," she mumbled. "Andrew and I *were* still friends, in the end. I don't know what changed his mind."

I didn't detect any malice from her. She clearly still had a sense of protectiveness towards Andrew even after his death. And Nick, come to that. But did that extend to covering up a murder?

Maybe the blood bank would give me some clues about who had bitten Andrew. If I knew that, it'd be easier to piece together the events that had led to his death.

11

I set out for the hospital on my lunch break after picking up a sandwich from Zee's place. I still felt uneasy walking around town alone, but with Jet gone, I had no way to contact Xavier. Estelle had had to take over Aunt Candace's usual job of updating the records since Aunt Candace had locked herself in her room and refused to come out. Apparently, she wasn't taking her breakup with Dominic particularly well. Cass was absent, too. Maybe it wasn't a bad idea to bring back Swift so she could say a proper goodbye. Or maybe she'd just laugh and call me soft again.

You'd think living in a library that disobeyed the basic laws of nature would make it easier to find my way around town, but I still got lost on the way to the hospital. My hands and feet were soon numb, the bitter winter air doing its best to freeze every inch of exposed skin.

"What are you doing?" Sylvester swooped down to land on my shoulder. I staggered under the unexpected weight of the large owl.

"Getting lost," I said through chattering teeth. "I thought you never left the library."

"I thought *you* never left the library alone," he said, digging his talons into my shoulder as he took off once more. "Since nobody else is present, I saw it as my duty to keep you alive."

"Why, Sylvester, I'd almost think you cared," I said. "I'm looking for the hospital, actually. Do you know where it is?"

"What, finally getting that head of yours looking at?"

"Ha ha," I said. "It's up to you. If you want to follow me while I walk in circles, be my guest."

"That does sound entertaining," he said. "You know, most people would look up directions *before* leaving."

"I'm aware of that," I said. "If you help me find the hospital, I'll let you watch when I summon Cass's kelpie back."

"You're doing *what?*" he said.

"Summoning Cass's kelpie," I said. "She's mad at me because he escaped without giving her the chance to say goodbye and she blames me for it. If I summon him back, I might get a moment's peace."

He howled with laughter. "I have to see that. Fine. To get to the hospital, turn left, right, left, and then keep straight on."

I kept his directions in mind and continued down the high street, debating what to ask at the blood bank. If they'd seen Andrew in person, then they must have known he wasn't one of their usual visitors. I mean, there were only so many teenaged vampires in town, right? If Andrew had robbed the place, on the other hand, they might not be able to help me.

"There." Sylvester indicated a tall brick building on the street corner. "Don't ever say I don't do you any favours."

Hmm. Maybe Sylvester did have a vested interest in keeping me alive. Or one of my aunts had put him up to this. Either way, I appreciated the company, now my own familiar had gone. I hadn't realised how much I'd miss the crow's presence until I spotted another crow perched on the hospital sign. It was smaller than Jet, though, and took flight when Sylvester perched self-importantly on the sign to wait for me.

I walked through the glass doors into the hospital and nearly collided with Dominic walking the other way.

"Oh, hey," I said. "Ah—were you at the blood bank."

"Yes, I was," he said, looking me up and down. "Why, have you decided to join us in our eternal night?"

"No," I said. "Eternal night? Seems a bit overdramatic. What's wrong?"

"I may," he said, "have made a terrible mistake."

"What, breaking up with my aunt?" I looked around in case anyone was eavesdropping, but the receptionist didn't even look up. It seemed that vampires making dramatic statements wasn't a noteworthy occurrence. "Never mind. I was going to ask if the blood bank had misplaced a large number of bottles lately."

"Funny you should say that," he said. "Last week, in fact. Why?"

"Andrew Lynch," I said. "He stole them. Don't you have people guarding the blood supplies?"

"Not vampires, no," he said. "Blood isn't hard to come by, in a place like this."

Uh... that wasn't creepy at all. "Should I report it? I suppose his parents probably threw the bottles away if they found them."

"Do whatever you like," Dominic said, walking around me. "I wash my hands of your family, forever."

"I thought you regretted your decision." I spun on the spot, expecting him to pull another of his disappearing acts, but he stopped mid-walk.

"Regret doesn't mean it wasn't the right choice to make," he said. "Your aunt is… difficult."

"That's one word I'd use," I said. "If Andrew stole the bottles of blood from here, does that mean nobody saw him? Because he wasn't a vampire until recently."

"It's the blood bank's policy not to ask questions," he said, showing a flash of fangs. "I'm sure you can guess why they're reluctant to pry."

"Um, but isn't it illegal to turn someone into a vampire?" I asked. "If Andrew really was a vampire, someone other than him broke the law. Isn't Evangeline looking into that?"

"I haven't the faintest idea," he said.

"Wait," I said, seeing him shift his weight, about to leave. "One quick question—confidential, mind. Don't tell anyone."

"Oh?" He raised an eyebrow.

With a glance over my shoulder, I thought, clearly, *If a vampire was attacked by a Reaper's scythe, what would happen to their soul?*

His eyes widened. And then in a flash, he was gone.

"Dominic!"

"What're you yelling at?" Sylvester said. "Are you done? I'm freezing my feathers off here."

"Yeah, I guess I'm done," I said, defeated. There was no point in asking the hospital about the stolen blood, not without admitting I'd snooped around Andrew's room. I didn't want to bring any more trouble to his family.

"Now it's time for you to bring back the kelpie," he said. "You *are* going to keep your word, right?"

"Yes." I was starting to think I'd made a mistake with Dominic in telling him about my Reaper theory, even if I hadn't said a word aloud. He might be the most trustworthy vampire I knew, but if the theory was true, all evidence pointed to Nick being more dangerous than he seemed. Even if he was the type of person who'd break into the vampires' headquarters at night, just how had he outwitted the Reaper?

Sylvester kept up a stream of 'encouraging' comments as I

walked to the beach. I tuned him out, but the closer I got to the sea, the more ridiculous an idea it seemed. Cass *would* laugh at me, I was sure.

Still, I had to admit I missed Swift's company, too. If I could call him back, then maybe I'd be able to do the same for my own familiar.

I slowed as I reached the seafront, notebook and pen in hand. The tide was in, preventing me from standing on the beach, so I made for the pier instead. On windy days like today, most of the pier was closed off to prevent anyone from being swept into the sea. I stopped beside the fenced-off area and saw a blond head bobbing above the water's surface.

"What's he doing out there?" Sylvester snorted. "Your boyfriend has a death wish. I suppose he *is* Death, so maybe his goal is to end up hoisted on his own scythe."

"What are you doing?" I called to Xavier, ignoring the owl.

Xavier looked up and waved. He really shouldn't be able to swim with the weight of the scythe strapped to his back. Another perk of being a Reaper.

Xavier swam up to the side of the pier. "I'm looking for the missing soul again."

"Ah—I had a theory on that," I said. "But first, I have something else I wanted to do."

He frowned. "Oh?"

"Summon the kelpie," I said. "I don't know if my magic will work this far from the library, but if it gets Cass to leave me alone, I'll do it."

He pulled himself out of the water onto the pier's wooden planks, scythe and all. "I won't stop you, but are you sure?"

"I'm sure." I pressed my pen to the page and wrote, *Swift,* focusing as hard as I could on the image of the kelpie in my mind.

"I don't think it's working," said Sylvester. "Why don't you try jumping into the water and doing an interpretive dance?"

"Don't be a downer," said Xavier. "What're you doing here, anyway?"

"Keeping an eye on Rory," said the owl. "I thought that was *your* job, but I suppose if I had to watch her all the time, I'd take off for a swim, too."

"Ignore him," I said. "I got curious about how Andrew got hold of all that blood, so I went to the hospital to check it out and ran into Dominic."

"How *did* he get hold of all the blood?" asked Xavier.

"Stole it, apparently." I shook my head. "Because half the academy students are aspiring thieves—"

A wave rose from the sea, crashing over us. Xavier grabbed my shoulders, not a moment too soon. I staggered backwards as a torrent of water filled my mouth, and salt stung my eyes. Gasping, I spat water out and pushed a hunk of sopping hair out of my face in time to see the kelpie leave the sea in a flying leap and gallop along the seafront.

"Oh, no," I spluttered. "I didn't—I should have brought Cass here."

"Imbecile!" shrieked Sylvester. "You killed me. Murderer!"

"You aren't dead," said Xavier, who looked unruffled despite the drenching. His golden hair was bone-dry, and so was his hand when he let go of me.

I shook my notebook and reached for my pen. It was lucky I hadn't dropped either of them. Carefully, I wrote *dry,* and the water vanished from my clothes and hair. "Good. I didn't make every drop in the ocean vanish."

"I wouldn't put it past you," said Sylvester. "You *monster.*"

"Sorry," I said. "I didn't mean to."

"You have seaweed stuck in your feathers," said Xavier. "Let me help."

Sylvester huffed, but let him pull the clump of seaweed

off his wing. As he did so, a scrap of waterlogged paper fell off. Xavier caught it in his hand and made to throw it away.

"Wait, what is that?" I asked.

"A receipt from the apothecary."

"That's where Nick stole the firedust from," I said. "I—oh, no. Stop that!"

Swift galloped right in front of the police station, spraying the windows with water.

"I might as well hand myself over for arrest right now." I broke into a run, sprinting off the pier and on the kelpie's tail. The giant water horse whipped around the corner past the clock tower and continued full-tilt towards the town square.

I pelted across the road and ran into the square in time to see Swift stick his head into Zee's bakery and emerge with a muffin in his mouth.

"Ah, sorry!" I yelled at Zee.

"Don't worry, I gave it to him this time." She emerged from the bakery, grinning. "This is the most entertainment I've had in weeks."

Apparently, she wasn't the only one who thought so. A growing crowd gathered on the outskirts of the square, shoppers watching the chaos in groups. The kelpie turned on the spot, his magnificent white-blue mane swinging.

I realised where he was going the instant he moved. Breathless, I grabbed my notebook and pen and wrote the word *stop!*

Swift skidded to a halt, inches from the library doors, knocking a student flying in the process. The boy picked himself up, groaning.

"Oh, sorry, Cameron," I said.

"Ow," he said, looking at the kelpie with a panicked expression on his face. "Have you seen—there you are."

A crow flew past and landed on his head.

"I didn't know you had a crow familiar," I said.

"I didn't know you had a kelpie."

"He's not mine." And I should have brought Cass to the beach rather than setting him loose in town again. I'd assumed he'd decided to pursue a life at sea, but maybe he did miss the library. Or just Zee's muffins. Swift nuzzled my hand and I stroked his head.

"Looks like he is," commented Cameron, backing away from both of us.

I ran a hand down the kelpie's back, and he let out a soft neigh. *Okay, maybe he does still like me.* Swift had come to trust me in the weeks I'd helped Cass take care of him, but I'd assumed I'd blown that trust when I'd shut him in the cage.

Sylvester swooped over my head. "What now, genius?"

"Sylvester, would you please fetch Cass? She'll be disappointed if I have to send him back to sea without her having the chance to see him first."

"No need," he said, pushing the door open. "She's already here."

Sure enough, Cass herself emerged seconds later. Her eyes widened at the sight of the kelpie standing there on the doorstep, letting me stroke him. "Goddess, what have you done now?"

To my surprise as much as Cass's, everyone in the square applauded at her appearance. They'd moved closer, forming a circle to watch us.

Cass shook her head at me. "You brought him back?"

"I had to use a spell to get him to keep still," I said. "Since I removed the amplifying spell someone *accidentally* put on my notebook, I managed to stop him without any issues."

Her face flushed. "You shouldn't have used magic on him."

"If I hadn't, he'd have got loose in the library," I said. "Not going to thank me?"

"Don't!" yelled Sylvester. "She and that monster almost drowned me."

"Oh, you be quiet." Cass walked to Swift's side. He lowered his head, allowing her to stroke him. "Can one of you tell those people to find someone else to stare at?"

"Hey, you're giving them a great show." I dug my hand in my pocket and found my notebook. "When did you do it, anyway?"

"What?"

"The notebook, Cass." I rolled my eyes. "I'm done playing games with you, but if you're breaking into my room while I'm not there—"

"No, you left it on the desk after you got drenched when Swift escaped, idiot."

So I had. "You sneak."

"You made it too easy." She stroked the kelpie. "By the way, your boyfriend looks peeved."

"He's not my—" I spotted Xavier waving at me across the square. Ignoring Cass's snort, I walked to join him. A few people glanced our way, but most of them were more interested in Swift.

"My boss is calling me," Xavier said. "Will you be okay handling the kelpie?"

"I think Cass has the situation in hand," I said. "I had something I wanted to tell you before this happened. Alone."

"Oh. Sure." There was nowhere safe to talk without a bunch of curious onlookers, but if I didn't tell him about the thief, it might be too late. "Can I drop by later? Give it an hour, the crowd will be gone."

"Actually, can I come back with you? This is something the Reaper needs to hear, too."

His brows shot up. "Okay, sure."

My heart raced at the very idea of speaking to the Reaper. Perhaps he wouldn't believe anyone would dare to steal his scythe—and for all I knew, it *wasn't* possible for anyone to have done it. But the only way to know for sure was to catch the killer.

I did my best to ignore the stares as we headed past the clock tower to the seafront again. Even Xavier's confident manner seemed tense, and I waited until we were out of earshot of the square before saying, "I think I know how Andrew died."

"Really?" he said.

"Yeah, it hit me last night when we caught Nick and his friends stealing from the vampires," I admitted. "I should have mentioned it then."

"Don't worry about it," he replied. "What do you think?"

"I think they stole from the Reaper instead," I said. "Andrew's soul was gone, right? And you thought another Reaper might have come onto your turf. But what if it wasn't a Reaper, but someone else using his scythe?"

His eyes darkened. "What, you think my boss *wasn't* paranoid?"

"I don't know what to think," I said quietly. "All I know is that Andrew's soul disappeared, and the main suspect is reckless enough to try to steal from the leader of the vampires. Andrew himself was a thief—he stole from the blood bank, too. I don't know how else his soul could have disappeared, but I'm not the expert here."

"Yes," he said, half to himself. "You're right, but... I have a suspicion that my boss will require more proof before he'll even consider the possibility of a human getting the best of him."

I thought so. I quickened my pace as we turned into the high street, which was unusually empty for this time of day. Probably because everyone was at the square watching Cass and Swift. Except for...

Xavier stopped walking. So did I. A body lay sprawled at the roadside, sightless eyes staring up at us.

Dominic.

12

Xavier moved first, pacing around Dominic's inert body. His brow furrowed, his eyes seeming to dull in colour. I'd only seen him wearing that expression once before: when he'd been looking at a corpse to see where the soul was.

"His soul," said Xavier. "It's gone."

I clapped a hand to my mouth. "Oh, no. It's my fault."

"No, it isn't," he said.

"I told him my theory," I whispered. "Nobody else. The killer must have figured he'd spread the word to everyone and ambushed him so he couldn't warn the other vampires."

"How would the killer know you'd told him?" asked Xavier. "My guess is that he was trying to confront the thief himself and paid with his life. It wasn't your fault, not at all."

"He'd never have thought to do it if I hadn't put the idea in his head," I said, my throat closing up. "We have to call the police."

"I don't have a phone," he reminded me. "I'll make sure nobody moves the body."

"Ah." I dug my hand in my pocket, pulled out my phone

and gave it a shake. "Oh, no. It got drenched by that wave earlier. I think it's broken."

He swore. "Can you call your familiar?"

"Jet. I need you."

No response. Wait, calling him by name wouldn't work away from the library even if he wasn't mad at me.

Instead, I pulled out my notebook and pen with shaking hands. The pages were crumpled from the soaking they'd had, but the pen's magical ink was as bright as ever. I wrote a single word—*Jet.*

"I don't know if it'll work the same way it did for the kelpie," I admitted.

"Have more faith," he said. "He knows you need him."

"Partner!" screamed a voice, and the crow flew at me, crashing headlong into my face in a shower of feathers. Jet spun in a dizzying circle before landing beside Dominic's body. At that point, he let out a shriek. "He's dead, he's dead, he's dead!"

"Jet, calm down!" Maybe I should have called Sylvester instead. "Can you fetch the police, please? We can't let the killer come back."

"Danger!" he screamed. "Danger!"

"Well, that's one way to warn everyone," Xavier remarked.

Sure enough, by the time the crow took in my command to fly to the police station, people had started to emerge from the nearby shops.

"What happened here?" asked a tall thin man wearing a long, buckled cloak. A crooked pointed hat perched on his head. "Is he dead?"

"Yes, he is." My gaze snagged on the shop he'd just come out of. "You work at the apothecary, right? Uh, has anything disappeared from your stores lately?"

"Funny you should say that," he said. "There's been a number of thefts this week. I can't imagine what someone's plotting to do with invisible ink, firedust, and half my ingredients stock. The same thief stole a set of antique vampire fangs from Flanders' Antique Shop, too."

"They stole—what?" Perplexed, I looked at Xavier, seeing my own confusion reflected in his eyes. Why would anyone feel the need to steal a pair of fangs? Unless... they wanted to fake a vampire attack to cover up a murder.

A chill raced down my back. If it was true, maybe Andrew hadn't been a vampire at all. Then again, Dominic hadn't been able to read his mind. Something didn't add up.

By the time Edwin hurried over, we'd drawn a wide crowd, making it impossible for me to question the owner of the apothecary. When a group of witches nearly trod on Dominic's limp arm, I moved it out of the way and a crumpled piece of paper fell out of his hand. I read the first word —Rory—and quickly hid it up my own sleeve.

He left me a note.

"What is going on?" bellowed Edwin.

The crowd parted to let him through, and he stared down at Dominic's body with undisguised fear.

I leaned closer to Xavier. "Are we going to tell him who we suspect? Because we don't know *where* the killer went. And if he resists arrest, more people might get hurt or worse."

How did you defend yourself against a Reaper's scythe, even wielded by an inexperienced human? I didn't know, and from Xavier's uneasy silence, he didn't either.

"I'll take care of it," Xavier finally said, approaching Edwin. "May I speak to you in confidence?"

"No, you may not," said the elf. "This is the second time you've shown up beside a body with Aurora Hawthorn. Let me guess—he is without a soul, too."

"Correct," Xavier said. "If you refuse to listen to me in

confidence, then allow me to state who I suspect: Nick. Possibly, he worked with his accomplices, Gail and Zach."

A murmur rippled through the crowd.

"They're kids," said Edwin. "They have already been questioned, besides, and had an alibi for the first murder."

"You might want to check that again," I said. "They're carrying something… something you want to know about. Trust me."

Xavier dropped his voice. "The suspected killer is carrying a very dangerous weapon. If anyone other than a Reaper confronts them, it's likely to end fatally."

Edwin's gaze darted to Xavier, then to his hands as he subtly moved his scythe so the elf could see it.

"Yes…" Edwin's voice was faint. "I see, Reaper. If that's the case, then I would like to speak with you alone. Am I right in assuming that Aurora Hawthorn's part in this is over?"

"Hey—" I began, but Xavier nodded.

"Yes, it is. I'd suggest everyone else leave, too," added the Reaper.

The crowd stirred, parting as Edwin's troll guards made their presence known.

I caught Xavier's arm, whispering, "What if he doesn't have the weapon on him? He might have hidden it. Or even returned it like last time."

Which didn't make a great deal of sense, but Nick hadn't started out with the intention of committing murder. I didn't think so, anyway. But now two people were dead, and someone would have to break the news of Dominic's death to Aunt Candace. *Oh, no.*

"I should confront him alone, Rory," he said. "Best not to put yourself at risk."

"I don't want you to risk your own life, either. Even if you know, you're not alive in the usual sense."

He gave a faint smile. "I'll take that as a compliment. You

should leave—I'll see you later when this sorry business is dealt with."

I didn't manage a smile back. Rationally, I knew there was nothing I could have done to save Dominic. But had he really gone after the killer alone, or had the killer stalked him after overhearing our conversation at the hospital? I could have sworn there hadn't been anyone close enough to overhear, least of all Nick. He'd been at the library at the time.

"Evangeline is on her way," I heard Edwin say, and I shuddered inwardly. I didn't want to be here when she and the other vampires found out Dominic was dead.

As I walked away, I unfolded the note I'd hidden up my sleeve. The message Dominic had meant to give to me.

Rory. Don't show her the journal.

————

The words of Dominic's last note bounced around my head for the rest of the day. I assumed 'she' was Evangeline, but what did my journal have to do with anything? Perhaps Dominic had planned to hand me the note with an explanation later on, and he hadn't expected to be ambushed first. But since he was dead and none of the other vampires even knew the journal existed aside from their leader, there was nobody I could turn to for guidance.

Besides, we had bigger problems. The moment Aunt Adelaide broke the news of Dominic's death to her sister, Aunt Candace had lost it. Black drapes now adorned everything in the library from the balconies to the shelves. And if that wasn't enough to scare off the patrons, her wailing echoed downstairs from our living quarters in an endless out-of-tune dirge. Even Sylvester and Jet had flown outside to avoid the racket.

"Can't someone use a muting spell?" I said to Estelle as we

sorted through the books the fleeing students had left in the Reading Corner. "There must be one."

"Not when she's using the library's own magic to get her point across." Estelle winced as Aunt Candace hit a particularly high note with the finesse of a mallet striking a brick. "She'll run out of steam soon."

"Not soon enough. It's been two hours." I rubbed my ears. "Why is Cass allowed to skive off and not us?"

"Because she said she'd bring the kelpie into the library if she had to help out." Estelle slid another book into place.

"Might distract Aunt Candace for a bit." I covered my ears at the sound of another strident wail. "She didn't even thank me for it."

"She's Cass. She'll show her thanks by being one percent nicer to you."

"One percent is better than zero." I continued sorting books, stacking them in piles according to which floor they came from. "I can't focus with that racket going on."

"You don't have to," said Aunt Adelaide, appearing from behind a bookshelf with a long-suffering expression on her face. "Deal with the books later. We're closing for the day."

"What if all the people in the square want to come in?" asked Estelle.

"Pretty sure most of them will have gone home by now," I said. Or followed Cass to the beach to watch her say goodbye to Swift.

"Exactly," said Aunt Adelaide. "You both deserve the rest of the day off."

"Okay," said Estelle, standing. "We'll pick it up when Aunt Candace calms down. Maybe we should see if Cass is okay."

"I think Cass is fine." I raised my voice as Aunt Candace wailed again. "She doesn't have to listen to this."

"Nor do I," said Aunt Adelaide, irritably. "I'm going to employ an earplug charm, and I suggest you do the same."

She waved her wand, then walked away.

"I don't know that spell," I said.

"I can teach you," Estelle said. "Then you can chill out and read a book for a while. I think you need to."

"You know… for once in my life, I don't feel like doing that." I sighed. "I know Xavier has the investigation in hand, but still, the killer's out there with a dangerous weapon."

"Isn't that a good reason *not* to leave the library?" she said. "I'd prefer not to be around when the Reaper confronts him for stealing his scythe."

Estelle had taken my explanation more calmly than I'd expected, but she seemed confident the police would catch Nick in no time. Aunt Adelaide was, too.

"Is he likely to do that?" I said. "I thought the police were the ones who decided his punishment."

"Maybe," she said. "I've never heard of anyone stupid enough to steal from the *Reaper* before. That kid has some nerve."

"More like no common sense." Apparently, he hadn't learned from what I'd said to him last night at all.

"Partner!" squeaked a voice. Jet flew over to me, landing on my shoulder. "Partner, your aunt is very upset! Does she want company?"

Estelle let out a small laugh, stifling it with her hand. She probably thought the same as me… the last thing Aunt Candace needed was Jet chattering away at her while she was grieving.

"Uh… no," I said. "She wants to be left alone."

"Oh." He shuffled his feathers. "Do you, too?"

I winced at the sound of another screech. "No, but I'm going to find somewhere quieter. Can you see if the police have caught Nick yet?"

"Of course!" he said, flying towards the door.

"I'm glad you two made it up," Estelle said to me. "So

you're keeping the spell active, then? I thought it wasn't meant to be permanent."

"It wasn't," I said. "But the amplifying spell was still active when I used it."

"I can't believe Cass," she said, shaking her head. "That explains how you made all that water disappear. Don't tell her I said this, but I think locking her in the cage with the manticore was entirely justified. She's the one who smuggled it in here, besides."

"Hmm," I said. "I could erase the familiar spell, but that might upset him again. Besides, I kind of like having a familiar I can talk to. I guess I just need to find someone he can natter away to when I'm busy."

"That would have been punishment enough for Cass," said Estelle. "I can't listen to this a moment longer. Want to do the earplug spell?"

"Sure." I dug my hand in my pocket and Dominic's note fell out. "Ah—forgot about this. Dominic was holding it when he died."

"Wait, what is that?"

I held out the note. "I know I should have handed it over to the police, but I don't want everyone to know about the journal."

"What…" She stared at the note. "Don't show… who?"

"If I had to guess, I'd say he meant Evangeline, the vampires' leader."

Her eyes bulged. "Why, does he think *she* might want to steal it?"

"I don't think now's a good time to ask her if it's true." I crumpled the note in my hand. "Or if it's linked to his murder, come to that. I… I don't know what to think."

Was the killer connected to the vampires who'd tried to steal the journal? No evidence suggested he was, but if it was true, the whole town might be in danger.

A clap of thunder sounded, drowning out Aunt Candace's wail. Then a drop of rain fell from the high ceiling, followed by another.

"Wait, is she making it rain?" I said.

"Oh no," said Estelle. "Aunt Candace, stop!"

Another clap of thunder sounded, then a deluge of rain poured down, drenching both of us in an instant. I shoved a handful of sopping wet curls out of my face and fumbled in my pocket for my notebook.

Thunder crackled, then lightning speared the library down the centre. Aunt Candace's wailing filled the background like an orchestra of nightmares.

"Make it stop!" yelled Estelle, grabbing her own notebook. "Stop—"

The rain continued to pour even as she scribbled frantically. I pressed the tip of my pen to the page, racking my brain for any word likely to make the thunderous weather stop. After a pause, I wrote *amplify.*

Then, *dry.*

The rain stopped in an instant, every drop of water vanishing from our clothes and my now considerably crumpled notebook.

Estelle gaped at me. "How did you do that?"

I grinned. "Thanks to Cass, I know how to give my magic a boost. I wouldn't try showering until it gets fixed, though."

"Small price to pay," she said.

"Yeah." I'd almost rather deal with the vampires than Aunt Candace today.

A snowflake fell, followed by another.

"Oh, no," said Estelle.

"How'd she even do that?" I said.

"She's using the library's magic," Estelle said, wearing an alarmed expression. Her hair was tangled from the drenching we'd both got. "Let's get out of here."

"Agreed."

We reached the door as the snowflakes swirled into a blizzard, escaping into the town square. I inhaled the fresh sea breeze, relieved at the pleasant silence outside the doors. It might be freezing, but at least there wasn't a snowflake in sight.

"Let's find Cass," said Estelle.

"Or Jet," I put in. The police station was on the seafront, anyway. If Nick had been arrested, then that was where we'd find him.

But what if he wasn't the person who'd stolen the scythe?

13

The square was deserted, for once. Estelle and I hurried along, our newly re-dried cloaks swirling around our ankles. Most of the shops were still open, but there was no sign of the kelpie. I spotted Alice from the pet shop closing up for the evening.

"Hey," she said as we passed by. "Are you looking for your sister? She went to the beach with that giant horse of hers."

"Thought so," I said. "Did you hear about the vampire being murdered?"

Her cheery manner vanished. "Yeah, I saw Edwin's trolls taking those three kids to the police station."

"Wait, they caught the killer?" I glanced at Estelle, who also looked surprised. "Uh—was he carrying anything?"

Alice's brow furrowed. "I don't know, I didn't see. Why?"

"Never mind." I took a step backwards. "I think we'd better go and find Cass."

"You mean, go to the jail," Estelle muttered to me as we left Alice behind. "That's what you're really up to, isn't it?"

"Maybe," I admitted. "I don't know, something still

doesn't add up. The scythe… why would he go to the trouble of stealing it again only to give himself up?"

"Guilty conscience?" she suggested. "Let's face it, a giant scythe's difficult to hide. Anyone might have spotted him."

"You'd think so." But a nagging doubt in the pit of my stomach pursued me all the way to the seafront.

"Doesn't look like the Grim Reaper's in there, at least," Estelle said, as we drew closer to the police station.

"Have you ever met the guy?" I asked her.

She shook her head. "No, but rumour has it he's worse than Evangeline when he's in a temper."

A chill swept down my spine. I'd seen a hint of what Xavier was capable of with his Reaper powers, but he'd never used them around me, and it was easy to forget he wasn't human. The Grim Reaper, on the other hand, might not stop to ask questions before unleashing his scythe on anyone who got in his way.

What if they *had* arrested the wrong person?

The police station was packed. Estelle and I squeezed through the doors into the lobby, with difficulty. It looked like half the academy students' parents had shown up.

"Look, you're welcome to search our house," said Nick's mother, who wore the same hat as the previous night but had a dark pink cloak on instead of a dressing gown. "There's no scythe hidden anywhere on our property. My son is not the killer you're looking for."

"Neither is my daughter!" said a red-haired witch. She wore a lime green coat and a frantic expression. "There's been a mistake."

"No mistake," said Edwin. "Your son's actions last night prove that he is the most likely suspect for any crime against the vampires, and he gave himself up willingly."

"My son is a thief, but he's not a killer," insisted Nick's mother. "This is absurd. He's sixteen years old. He might have made a foolish mistake last night, but he's learnt the error of his ways. He's a teenager, not a master criminal."

"Teenagers can be master criminals," said Edwin. "I'm terribly sorry about your son, but he will be tried as a minor, once we find the property he has stolen and return it to its rightful owner. As the scythe is hidden in a location only the thief knows, we cannot possibly let him walk free."

I looked at Estelle. "I don't think we're much help here."

"No, but they have a point. Where *is* the scythe?"

I don't know. The doubt buzzing inside me had multiplied into a swarm, and I shifted uncomfortably from one foot to the other. "Either Nick hid it somewhere, or the killer still has it and they've arrested the wrong person."

"Even she agrees with me," said Nick's mother, and I wished I hadn't said anything. The elf's face turned red, all the way to the tips of his pointed ears.

"There's a procedure," Edwin said. "I must ask you to calm down, Mrs Anders."

"How can a teenager possibly have killed a vampire?" said a tall, thin man wearing a suit who I assumed must be Nick's father. "Anyone would have heard him coming."

He had a point. Even if Dominic hadn't been paying attention, it wouldn't be hard for his vampire senses to pick up on Nick's approach. And if Dominic *had* seen him, then his mind-reading power would have given away Nick's movements before he'd had the chance to use the scythe. A teenager wasn't a match for a vampire who could move at an inhuman speed *and* read his mind.

The door opened behind us, and a hush momentarily fell over the crowd. The trolls shrank back, hiding behind one another, as Evangeline strode in, her dress billowing around her ankles.

My pulse started to race. I'd thought she'd already been to the crime scene.

"Where," she demanded, "is Dominic?"

A pale-looking Edwin indicated a door on the left-hand side of the lobby, and everyone tripped over their feet in an attempt to get out of Evangeline's way. Even the troll guards looked utterly terrified, their huge bodies quaking in fear. She disappeared through the door, and the entire room seemed to hold its breath.

A few moments later, Evangeline emerged from the room. "Where, exactly, is the murder weapon?"

"We have yet to determine that," said Edwin, his voice fainter than usual.

"It was stolen," Xavier added. "By the killer."

Evangeline scanned the crowd, her gaze penetrating. As though she was probing everyone's minds for everything they knew about the missing scythe. Dominic's note came to mind, and I pushed the thought away. I didn't want her to see it. I didn't want her to see any of my thoughts, in fact.

I focused on a crack in the wall and kept my gaze there. Every time she looked my way, I fixed my thoughts on the crack in the wall and nothing else.

A frown puckered her brow, and she looked at me again, this time making no effort to disguise it. I kept thinking about the gap in the wall, pushing all wayward thoughts of Dominic, the journal, and the murder aside. Evangeline shifted her gaze away, and the air itself trembled with tension.

"You all have nothing to say?" she asked, her voice deceptively soft and calm. "If that's the case, then I will have to probe the suspects myself, Edwin. I'm sure you understand why."

I stood still, my heart thudding. I'd done it. I'd kept a vampire out of my mind. Not only that, I'd managed to avoid thinking about the journal at all. She wouldn't have brought it up in front of the others, but I'd escaped questioning. For now.

I looked away from her, trying to calm my breathing, and spotted Jet's small black shape flitting near the ceiling. *Right, of course he's here.* What with Evangeline's abrupt arrival, I'd forgotten I'd sent him to have a look around the police station.

"Are you sure?" Edwin asked.

"I am certain," said Evangeline. "I will speak with the suspect and I will read the truth from his mind if he won't speak it aloud."

"Of course," said Edwin, his voice slightly tremulous. "If that is what you desire."

"It is, if you don't mind," she said. "I'd prefer to find out who attacked one of my fellow vampires before anyone else gets hurt." Her words were cold, and I shivered, as though Aunt Candace had dumped a bucket of snow down my back. I hoped she was angry with the killer, not with me for shutting her out of my mind. I hadn't picked the best time, but Dominic's last wish had been for me to keep the journal from her. I wouldn't betray that. Nor would I let another vampire get hold of Dad's journal, not even their leader.

Evangeline walked after Edwin through a door at the back. Another uneasy silence followed, in which nobody seemed to know where to look. Several people slipped outside, apparently deciding their fear of the vampires' leader outweighed their curiosity.

Estelle fidgeted next to me. "Do you reckon she'll get answers?"

"If he's the killer? He won't be able to hide it," I said. "He won't be able to hide where he put the scythe, either."

"For all our sakes, I hope he *did* do it," Xavier murmured, approaching me. "What are you two doing here? I thought you were going back to the library."

"Aunt Candace isn't taking Dominic's death well," I whispered back. "We came here until she calms down. Is the Reaper looking for the scythe?"

"No," said Xavier. "Not yet... and I hope for all our sakes that we track it down before that becomes necessary."

No kidding. Imagining the Grim Reaper and the leader of the vampires in a standoff made me feel even colder than before.

Seconds passed, each one dragging out. More people left, making the police station's lobby much less crowded. Finally, the only people left behind were the parents of the students who'd been arrested.

At that point, Edwin returned. "None of the people in this jail committed the murder," he announced. "All the arrested students will be freed."

"Good!" said Nick's mother. "He might be a bloody fool, but he's not a murderer."

Maybe—but then, who did it?

Evangeline strode through the lobby, giving me a cold, penetrating look on the way out. A fresh shiver of fear raced down my back. I hadn't given away anything with my thoughts, but she knew I'd been trying to keep her out of my mind.

Not that it mattered at this point. The killer walked free. Xavier moved to speak to Edwin, lowering his voice, while one of the trolls walked through the door at the back which presumably led to the jail. The other troll nervously watched the door as though expecting the leading vampire to come back in.

"I don't think she's coming back," Estelle said in comforting tones.

"Good," said the troll. "I don't like her. She gives me the creeps."

"Likewise," I said. "Here's a tip—if a vampire tries to read your mind, focus on something. Like a crack in the wall or the floor. Don't think of anything else. Then they won't be able to see your thoughts."

The second troll returned with the three students in tow. The red-haired girl was in tears. "It's my fault," she sobbed.

"No, it isn't," insisted her mother.

"Yes, it is," Gail gasped. "It was my idea to steal from the apothecary."

"It was?" The sound of Nick's mother yelling at him drifted past. "How—"

Estelle grabbed my arm. "We should get out of here."

"But—" I looked around for Jet, but the crow had disappeared. "Did you see where Jet went?"

"He was in here?"

"A minute ago." I moved towards Gail, who was still sobbing. "Excuse me, what did you steal?"

"Who are you?" asked her mother.

"I'm Aurora, from the library," I said. "I'm one of the people who caught her and Nick last night. Do you know anything else, Gail?"

Gail's mother moved in front of her daughter. "My daughter has been through a terrible ordeal. You're not with the police, are you?"

"Rory?" Xavier appeared at my side. "You should go. The killer's still out there, with the scythe, and they already killed one vampire."

"I know," I said. "But if it's not Nick, then who is it?"

"Whoever it is, they got the better of Dominic despite his mind-reading ability," said Xavier. "That suggests they're either a vampire, or they got really lucky."

"Partner!" shrieked a voice, and I turned around to find Jet fluttering at my side.

"There you are," I said. "You should go back to the library—"

159

"She is here, partner!"

"What in the goddess's name is going on?" demanded a voice.

I spun around to see Aunt Adelaide standing in the doorway, her cloak streaming behind her.

"Nothing's happening, Mum," Estelle said. "We couldn't find Cass—"

"Neither can I," said Aunt Adelaide. "Cass is missing."

"She was out on the pier with Swift." I gestured to the door. At least, that's where I assumed she'd gone. "Unless she went back to the library…"

"I didn't see her come in," said Aunt Adelaide. "I thought she'd come here with you or had got herself arrested for that stunt with the kelpie."

"No, Edwin's been busy dealing with the murder suspects," said Estelle. "Are you sure she didn't just go further down the beach with Swift?"

Xavier came over. "Rory, what's wrong?"

"Cass is missing," I said. "She was with the kelpie—"

"Gone, gone, gone," howled Jet, flying around my head.

"What is that racket?" Edwin said. "And what are you still doing in here?"

"My daughter is missing," Aunt Adelaide said. "Estelle, Rory—go back to the library. That's an order."

Estelle swore under her breath. "It's no use arguing with her when she's in this mood."

"I'll walk you back," Xavier said. "Trust me—it's best if you stay in the library until we find the real killer."

But Cass is missing. Sure, she might be a nuisance, but she was Estelle's sister and Aunt Adelaide's daughter, and despite her attempts to prank me on a daily basis, the time we'd spent with Swift had alerted me to the loneliness she tried to cover up. I felt an odd kinship with her at times, too.

What if the killer had taken her like he'd killed Dominic?

14

The library was deserted when we got back, but at least there was no sign of any snowflakes on any of the black-draped shelves. Mercifully, no wailing greeted us either.

"I think she's tired herself out," said Estelle.

"Or Aunt Adelaide managed to shut her up." I paced through the lobby. "Why didn't Aunt Adelaide let us go and look for Cass? We aren't any use back here."

"She's fine," Estelle insisted. "She was with Swift. Besides, there's no reason for the killer to have gone anywhere near her. She wasn't involved in the investigation."

"I was, though." Worry squirmed through me. "And don't forget Dominic died right after I told him my suspicions. I think the killer was listening when I talked to him at the hospital and realised I'd figured out he stole the scythe, so he decided to cover up his crime by committing another one."

"Maybe you're right," Estelle said, "but there's nothing any of us can do to *find* the scythe. Not even the Reaper can."

"We must be able to." I looked around at the endless

shelves. "Look, there's over a million books here, at least, right? One of them must be able to help us."

"Help us do what, track down the killer?" She frowned. "That's impossible if we don't know who it is."

"There's one way to narrow it down," I said. "The killer was spying on me at the hospital—maybe other times, too. They also sneaked up on Dominic and got the best of him despite his mind-reading skills. Is there a book in here that might tell me how that was possible?"

"I doubt that'll be in the general vampire textbooks," she said, her voice catching. "It'll be hidden deeper than that, and if we end up buried deep in the library, my sister… she…" Her voice broke on the last word, and I gave her a comforting hug, wishing I could do more.

Behind her, a stack of books on the front desk caught my eye. I knew how to get a more specific answer… if I was willing to take the risk.

I approached the desk, searching the shelf underneath. Sure enough, the book of questions was still there, its cover blank and deceptively innocuous.

"What are you doing?" Estelle rubbed her eyes. "Rory, that book is way too dangerous. Last time—you're lucky you got out."

"Maybe, but last time I asked the wrong question. Now I know what I want to ask it." At least, I thought I did.

"It's still risky," she said. "Only one person can go in at a time, and—and you might get stuck there for hours. Anything might happen."

"I know." I held up the book. "But the killer might have Cass, and I can't think of any other way to find him. Where's Sylvester, anyway?"

"Good question." Estelle faced the library and called out, "Sylvester? Where are you?"

"Partner!" howled Jet, flitting behind me. "Don't go, don't go!"

"Don't worry about me," I said to him. "You wait here, okay? Estelle and I—"

"We'll both go in," she said. "If one of us gets the question wrong, the other might still have a chance."

"But we get only one shot each." My nerves spiked. What if I asked wrongly, again, and ended up in even worse trouble than last time? I'd never catch the killer then. "Don't ask who the killer is. That's the question that got me thrown out last time."

"All right." Estelle opened the book, and said, "I wish to enter the forbidden room."

The pages glowed, and she vanished. Jet shrieked and flew around my head. "Gone, gone, gone."

"Jet, can you go and find Sylvester?" I was nervous enough without adding the crow's panicking on top of it. The book continued to glow but showed no signs of what might be happening to Estelle on the other side. I stepped from one foot to the other, my heart beating fast.

Then the glow dimmed. A moment later, Estelle reappeared, landing face-down on the lobby floor, soaking wet. "Ow."

"Are you okay?" I ran to her side.

"I am, but... but I got it wrong." Her face crumpled. "I asked where the killer took Cass. The room filled with water, and then I fell out."

"Ah." I reached for the book, my hand shaking a little. "Okay, I'm going to ask my question."

Estelle pulled her Biblio-Witch Inventory out and dried off her clothes, while I held up the book.

"I wish to enter the forbidden room."

As the book flew open, I tumbled into nothingness. This time, I'd expected it, but I still cringed when my knees buckled underneath me as I landed in the small square room. The walls were all painted black, the same as before, giving a cave-like impression.

Sucking in a breath, I asked, "If I wanted to stop a vampire from reading my mind, what would I do?"

Silence followed. Then the room started spinning, the walls blurring. I closed my eyes, a spike of nausea rising, and when I opened them again, Dominic stood in front of me.

I gasped. "You're dead."

"Yes, I am," he said. "Would you prefer me to take on another form?"

Dominic blurred, and the next second, Evangeline faced me. She wore a long lacy black dress, as elegant as she was in real life.

I stared. "Who *are* you?"

"I am the question room," said Evangeline. "Interesting. You could have asked any question, yet you picked that one. Why?"

"How do you—wait, are *you* reading my thoughts?"

"You belong to the library," said Evangeline. "I know how you think."

"That's really creepy," I said. "Are you going to answer my question?"

"Maybe," she said. "Maybe I'll decide you're unworthy first."

"Have you been taking lessons from Sylvester on how to be annoying?" I probably shouldn't provoke her, but there was no time to waste. Cass was gone, the Reaper's weapon was missing, and the person I'd been sure was the culprit had had nothing to do with the crime.

Evangeline transformed into Cass. "Maybe I have."

"Can you please just answer the question," I said. "My cousin's been kidnapped, and as long as the thief is on the loose, anyone might fall victim to the Reaper's scythe."

"Is that so?" said Cass. "And you think you're good enough at magic to pull off a rescue?"

"I never said that," I said. "I just wanted an answer to my question. Aunt Adelaide's out there looking for Cass, and the Reaper, but it'll be a lot easier if I can figure out who it is."

"You know who it is." Cass turned into Aunt Adelaide.

I shook my head. "I have an idea, but I want to know *how* the killer got the best of a vampire. Even with a scythe, how did he avoid having his thoughts read? For that matter, how did Andrew, if he never turned?"

Aunt Adelaide disappeared, and in her place stood Mortimer Vale.

"Hey, that's not on," I said, taking an automatic step back.

"You're afraid," said Mortimer softly.

"I'd be mad not to be," I said. "How'd he hide his thoughts, then? A spell or a potion?"

"Wrong question," said Mortimer, his soft voice sending a quiver down my spine.

"Who *are* you?" I forced myself to keep my eyes on his face. *It's not really him.*

"Someone who would prefer it if you didn't put yourself in harm's way, though damnation knows why."

I squinted at him, frowning. "You know, you really do remind me of Sylvester. He didn't come when Estelle called him."

"I imagine he's avoiding that annoying familiar of yours," said Mortimer, no longer sounding like himself.

"Oh my god," I said. "You *are* Sylvester. You sound just like him."

"Curses!" Mortimer Vale vanished, and in his place was the owl. "And I hoped you'd mess it up like last time."

I gaped at the tawny owl sitting on the floor. "*You're* the person who answers the questions? Is that why you're not a normal familiar?" How was it possible for the owl to know everything the library did?

"I am *nothing* like a normal familiar," he said, in self-important tones. "I'm a superior being."

"Then why are you keeping the answers from me?" I asked.

"Because they won't give you the satisfaction you need," he said. "It is believed that there is a potion that can enable a human to hide their thoughts, but the exact details are unknown."

"A potion that can block mind-reading abilities?" It seemed impossible. It also seemed like something only the vampires would know about. "How *do* you know everything? Are you like a living encyclopaedia, or are *you* the library?"

"You're forcing me to break my rule," said Sylvester. "I don't appreciate it. One question only."

"You know Cass has been kidnapped," I said.

"Yes, I do," he said in sour tones. "There's nothing either of us can do. I can't use an ounce of my power away from the library, and you're not capable of much better. As much as it pains me to admit it, I'd rather you not get yourself kidnapped, too."

"I'd prefer not to either, but at least I know what I'm up against," I said. "Aunt Adelaide doesn't, though. How can you not know everything about this potion that prevents mind-reading? I thought the library knew everything."

"Oh, nobody ever claimed that," said the owl. "The vampires have their own set of secrets, and that's the least of them. There are rumours about who possesses that information. I can't fathom how word spread to a human, but I can guess."

"Not..." I knew before he transformed again, into the tall, elegant vampire. "Mortimer Vale and his friends. Then... who? You know who the killer is?"

I was pretty sure I did, too, and now I was starting to see how he'd got the best of Dominic. Vampires relied on their mind-reading ability. The potion coupled with the element of surprise—not to mention the scythe—might have been enough to give the killer the edge. Because I'd told him my suspicion, the killer had felt compelled to cover his tracks. But that wasn't enough. He'd taken Cass, too, to remove my family from the picture for good.

Sylvester transformed into Evangeline again. "Now, why would Dominic have told you to hide the journal?"

"Because Evangeline is nosy and doesn't know when to stop probing into people's minds," I said. "That's not relevant, though, is it? Cameron is the one who stole the scythe. Why, I don't know, but he's dangerous and unhinged."

"All the better reason not to go out there alone, Rory," he said. "You can't help your cousin now."

"Says who?" Recklessness seized me. "If you don't let me out, I'll tell the entire town who you really are. You'll have a dozen people lining up to use the question room every hour and you'll never get a moment's peace again."

"You would never."

"I'm serious," I said. "I might not be the best witch out there—or even the best biblio-witch—but I don't abandon my family when they're in danger."

"Very well."

He vanished. The room disappeared, and then I was falling again, into empty darkness the colour of the walls.

The next second, I lay face-down behind the desk in the lobby.

Estelle gasped. "I thought you were trapped in there."

"Not quite." My head spun. I'd tell her about Sylvester later—tracking Cass was more important. I climbed to my knees, swallowing nausea. "I... I know who the killer is, but I don't know how he found out what he knows."

Evangeline? Surely not. She wouldn't have reason to tell a human how to get an advantage over a vampire.

"Who?" Estelle's eyes were wide.

"Cameron," I said grimly. "We knew it was a foolish academy student—but we guessed the wrong one. He has the scythe. Heaven knows why, but he took Cass to get at me. I know it's me he wants, because I'm the one who guessed he stole the scythe and told Dominic."

"You're not going after the killer, are you?" Estelle said. "Rory…"

"Jet," I said. "Have you seen another crow around? Cameron's familiar?"

"Another crow? Yes, yes, I saw him at the pier," said Jet.

"The pier," I said. "Of course. He must be out at sea somewhere… the other vampires can't cross the water."

Estelle's jaw dropped. "But—Cass was with Swift. He'd protect her."

"Cameron is carrying the Reaper's scythe," I reminded her. "I doubt Swift wanted to see Cass hurt."

"Don't risk your life, partner!" shrieked Jet.

"The other vampires can't cross the water," I said. "Someone else will have to stop him. For all I know, he's already stolen Cass's soul."

"And if you're not careful, he'll take yours too," said Estelle. "I'm not letting you go alone. My mum's out there—"

"And she wanted you to stay here," I said.

"How are you going to find him, Rory?" She shook her head. "He's in the middle of the ocean. You don't have a boat."

"I bet there's a spell, though," I said. "Right? Cass was going to use one to transport the kelpie to the sea the first time around, but she decided not to."

Estelle swore under her breath. "I want my sister back, too, but this isn't the right way to go about it."

"What else is there to do, leave her to die?" My voice

cracked. "If Aunt Adelaide catches up to him, who knows what he'll do to her?"

"Then I'm going with you," said Estelle.

I opened and closed my mouth. We'd wasted enough time already. "Sure, but—don't transportation spells only work on one person?"

"Yes, but I can teach you how to do it. You have to focus. Write, *travel* and focus on the person you want to get to."

I pulled out my notebook and pen. "Jet, can you please tell the police where we are?" I asked the crow, who let out a distressed chirp.

For a brief moment, I hesitated. Maybe I was losing my mind. Here I was, about to go out to sea to track down the criminal who'd decided the best place to escape justice was in the middle of the ocean. And who had a weapon that not even a vampire could stand up to.

But then again, I spent my days surrounded by the impossible.

I wrote the word *travel*, focused on the mental image of Cass, and the library disappeared.

15

Water crashed over my head. I gasped and spluttered, salt stinging my eyes. I blinked repeatedly, flailing my arms and legs. I'd landed in open water, too deep to touch the bottom. My vision cleared enough to show that Cameron sat on a sandy island only a few feet away. Beside him was Cass, and next to her lay Swift, half in and half out of the water. Her Biblio-Witch Inventory, notebook and pen lay in a pile, out of reach.

Estelle appeared next to me, crashing into the water with a gasp. Spluttering, she kicked out, grabbing my arm for balance. "We made it?"

Cameron was on his feet a moment later, the scythe in his hands. "You were supposed to come alone."

"You never said I had to." I swam until my feet touched the pebbled sand. Judging by the way the sea flowed around the island, he must have used some kind of spell to create it. "You can't stay out here forever. The police are looking for you." Or they should be, if Jet's warning had reached my aunt.

My heart missed a beat as his crow fluttered down to land

on his shoulder. I should have recognised that he wasn't Jet. "Don't move, either of you, or I'll take her soul."

"Idiot!" Cass yelled at us. "Why are you here?"

"To rescue you, obviously," I said. "Cameron, you don't have to do this. Think for a moment. You're stuck on an island with no provisions and no way to get back to the shore. All the vampires in town will be looking for you."

"They can't read my thoughts," he said. "They'll never see me coming."

"But does that mind-blocking potion have a time limit?" I asked. "It does, doesn't it? That's why you had Gail steal the ingredients from the shop for you."

It was a guess, but he instantly flushed. "What gives you the right to judge me?"

"You're holding my sister hostage and you as good as confessed to two murders," Estelle said. "Give it up."

"I won't." He swung the scythe, and I gasped, but he stopped inches from Cass's neck. "See? I'm the one in control here."

"But you're still afraid," I said. His hands were trembling on the scythe, and despite his confident tone, he must know I was right—he'd backed himself into a corner. "You know the vampires will take you to pieces when they catch you."

"There's nothing they can do to me," he insisted. "Not as long as I have this. The vampire I already killed didn't see me coming."

"But killing him wasn't enough, was it?" I said. "You wanted me gone, too, and that's why you took Cass."

"Yes, and you were stupid enough to take the bait," she shot at me.

"Do you want us to rescue you or not?" I stiffened as Cameron pointed the scythe directly at me.

"Nobody's getting rescued," he said. "You, Rory, get over here."

Estelle gave me an alarmed look, but the threat of the scythe got me moving. Until he let go of his weapon, we were all at his mercy.

"Where did you even find out about the potion?" I walked over to him, keeping both eyes on the scythe.

"Not that it's any of your business, but I read about it on the internet," he said.

I stopped. "The internet? Seriously?"

"Yeah, so?" he said defensively. "It's better than your library. I found a vampire online who was happy to answer my questions."

Hmm. "Did you tell this vampire your plan?"

"So what if I did?" He swung the scythe, and Estelle dodged out of the way just in time, dropping her Biblio-Witch Inventory in the process. *Oh, no.*

"Take out the notebook and pen and throw them over here, too," he said. "You too, Rory. And any wands or other bits of paper you might be carrying."

Cursing him silently, I dug in my pocket and tossed the notebook, pen and Biblio-Witch Inventory to join Estelle's and Cass's.

Swift gave a low growl but didn't move. He was trapped, too.

"Why'd you kill Andrew?" If I was going to die, I had nothing to lose by asking. "Was he the first person who stole the scythe?"

"Both of us," he said. "It was his idea. He promised to get himself turned into a vampire if I stole the Reaper's scythe. We were meant to be a team. But he faked it instead. Got cold feet. I nearly got killed by the Reaper, but he chickened out at the last minute. And then he tried to steal the scythe from me and got his own soul reaped in the process."

"Then you returned the scythe?" I surmised. "You didn't need to steal it again. Or kill Dominic."

"It's too late now." His grip tightened on the scythe. "I have to finish this."

There was a flash of black feathers as a crow landed on his shoulder, and as our eyes locked, I stared in surprise. It wasn't his pet crow, but Jet.

What're you doing here? It must have cost him some serious self-control to keep from speaking up and giving the game away.

Jet caught my eye. Then he screamed.

Cameron lost his grip on the scythe, startled, and Estelle made a lunge for her Biblio-Witch Inventory. She tapped a page, and Cameron flew backwards, splashing into the water.

The scythe fell, and I grabbed it before it could fall into the water, too. For a weapon almost as tall as I was, it was surprisingly lightweight. Like it weighed nothing, in fact.

Estelle fished the other notebooks and pens out of the pile and threw Cass hers. Cass, however, only had eyes for Swift. She murmured something to him, while Estelle handed me my props back.

"Thanks," I said, tucking the scythe under my arm so I could return them to my pocket.

Cameron emerged from the water, spluttering. "You're dead!" he yelled. "You're all dead. I won't give it back. I won't!"

"You *will* give it back," said a loud, resonant voice.

A shadow fell over the water, and the blood in my veins froze. Estelle stiffened, while even Cass stopped moving, remaining close to the kelpie.

Jet, meanwhile, flew to land on my shoulder.

"He's here," said Estelle, looking like she was about to faint. "The Grim Reaper."

The sea froze, every particle of water turning to ice. My teeth chattered, my hands trembling. Estelle was visibly shaking, too.

Then, the Reaper strode across the frozen ocean. He looked like a shadow shaped like a person, moving faster than any human had the right to. In seconds, he stood in front of me, extending a hand.

I held out the scythe, and he took it without a word of thanks. Then he advanced on Cameron. Estelle clutched my arm, quivering with fear.

Cameron screamed and tried to run, but the ocean was in the way. The Reaper picked him up and slung him over his shoulder.

The shadow shaped like a man turned away, Cameron still draped over his shoulder, and disappeared into nothingness.

Several long seconds passed before any of us spoke. "He's gone," I said. "He just took him."

"He deserved it." Cass stroked Swift's long mane, murmuring to him.

"Thanks, Jet." I held my hand out, and the crow hopped onto it, his little body trembling. "How'd you replace his familiar?"

"He flew away, Rory," he squeaked. "Most familiars never abandon their masters, but he did a despicable thing."

"If you can find him, I'm sure Alice will be able to get him a new witch or wizard to work with," said Estelle. "Someone who isn't a murderer."

"Yeah." I looked around at the sea lapping the edges of the sandy island. "Uh… how do we get back to shore?"

The water had unfrozen and judging by the fact that the fish swimming around us were still alive, the magic the Reaper had used hadn't done them any harm. Maybe the whole thing had been a trick.

He's scarier than the vampires. Even Evangeline.

"How do we get to shore?" said Cass. "By kelpie, of course."

"What—ride him?" I asked.

"If you do that, he'll throw you in the sea. No, watch."

She whistled, and the kelpie's ears perked up. Swift walked across the sand and into the water, the sea parting around his hooves.

"Neat trick," said Estelle. "How'd you get him to do that?"

"Just a little spell the two of us have been working on," Cass said smugly. "Well? Are you coming?"

We walked behind the kelpie towards the shore, all of us shivering in the aftermath of the Grim Reaper's magic. I tensed inwardly at the sight of a figure dressed in black and holding a scythe waiting on the beach, but relaxed when we drew closer and his golden hair became more obvious.

Xavier was an apprentice. When he became the Grim Reaper for real, would he end up looking like his master? Or was that what he actually looked like—inhuman?

"Rory!" he shouted my name, and something inside me seized up.

"I'm okay," I called back.

He wasn't alone. A crowd had gathered on the bank, including Aunt Adelaide, and even Aunt Candace—armed with her notebook and pen, of course.

"Are you sure?" Xavier met me on the path, taking my freezing hands in his. He felt human. For now, that's what I'd focus on.

"Sure," I said. "I will be, once I get back to the library."

He smiled. "I can arrange that."

16

Two days later, the library was closing up for the evening when the flutter of tawny wings overhead drew my attention from the box of books I was sorting.

"Sylvester?" I called, but the owl didn't respond.

I hadn't seen much of him since I'd unmasked him in the forbidden room. If I didn't know better, I'd say he'd been avoiding me. Jet, on the other hand, had hardly left my side. Since his frightening experience with the Reaper, he'd eased up on the chattering, though some of that was because whenever he wasn't with me, he was helping Aunt Candace in one of her late-night writing sessions by dictating the town's gossip to her.

I turned on the spot, searching for the owl. "Come on, I know you want to talk to me. You wouldn't go to the trouble of making me notice you if you didn't."

Sylvester fluttered down, landing on the desk in front of me. "You haven't undone your spell on the crow."

"Nope," I said. "If you're jealous, give it up. I'm not undoing it."

"Jealous? Never." He gave a sniff. "I'm far superior in intelligence."

"Yeah, well, you're the living embodiment of the library. Not all of us get to say that." I tilted my head. "Is that true? Do you know everything the library does?"

He was silent, which was answer enough in itself.

"Why do you still work for my aunt, then?" I asked. "How'd you end up like… this, anyway? Were you ever really an owl?"

"Ask your grandmother," he said.

"Uh, she's dead."

"I'm aware of that," said the owl. "If that's all—"

"I thought you wanted to talk to me," I said. "Let me guess: you want to know if I told anyone. And no, I didn't. Cass and Estelle don't know, right? Or Aunt Candace? Wait, Aunt Adelaide does, doesn't she?"

Silence. I turned to Jet, who said, "I won't tell."

"You'd better not," said Sylvester. "Your grandmother preferred everyone to see me as a familiar and an assistant."

"Why?" I asked. "For that matter, why can we only ask the forbidden room one question a day? Can't we just ask you in person?"

He fluffed his feathers. "It's impossible for one to hold the library's entire store of information in one's head at any given time, even for someone as intelligent as I am. I have to be inside the forbidden room to access that information."

"And that's why you couldn't tell me who the killer was," I surmised. "You also don't know about the vampires who want the journal, because even my aunts don't. Right?"

"Unfortunately," he said. "If I *did* know, then it would be easier to decide what to do about them."

"They're not coming here," I said. "Yet, anyway. It might not even have been one of those two who spoke to Cameron online."

"If it *was* them, then I hope you're making an effort to prepare yourself."

"Hey, I stopped Evangeline from reading my mind," I said. "And I held the Reaper's scythe, too."

"Rory's more of a hero than you are," Jet supplied.

"Really," said Sylvester, with a disgruntled look. "I could have helped her if I hadn't been stuck inside the library."

"You followed me outside the other day," I reminded him. Apparently, Jet helping me take down Cameron had hit his ego hard. Ah, well. "Don't worry, I won't tell a soul. Cameron is in jail where he belongs, so he won't be spreading the vampires' secrets around either."

But everyone knows the Reaper's scythe can kill them. Not that anyone else would be foolish enough to steal from him after his terrifying appearance on the beach.

Cameron had reappeared inside the jail an hour after he'd been taken, shaking and not speaking. Even Xavier had been surprised that the Grim Reaper hadn't taken his soul after all, but Cameron had been so scarred by the experience he'd run right into a jail cell and refused to come out.

I still had enough questions to fill a room, but Sylvester couldn't answer them. What *was* the journal, and why had Dominic not wanted me to show the vampires' leader? He was dead, so there was no chance of getting answers from him, but the question still nagged at me.

"Who are you talking to?" Estelle approached with her arms full of books. "Oh, Sylvester. There you are. I need to return this to the second floor."

"Gladly," he said, gripping the book in his talons and flying off with it.

"What were you two talking about?" asked Estelle.

"The vampires." I felt bad for keeping her in the dark about Sylvester's true nature, but maybe he'd be less keen to gang up against me with Cass if he knew I could reveal his secret at any time. "Dominic didn't trust Evangeline, and I might never know why. Not to mention what Cameron said —he spoke to a vampire on the internet who told him about the potion that blocks mind-reading. Doesn't that sound a bit like, well, those vampires are recruiting?"

"Not necessarily," said Estelle. "It might have been a one-off." But her tone suggested she didn't really believe it. The other vampires might not be in town, but they were still causing trouble. Lucky the Aspiring Vampires Society had permanently disbanded.

"I hope you're right."

Villain or not, I didn't trust Evangeline. Not a bit. But they didn't matter. I had the library, and I had my familiar. Okay, he might have a quirkier personality than I'd planned for, but life was never dull. Besides, someone had to listen to the patrons' chatter while they tried to make small talk with me.

The library door opened, and Cass walked in, carrying a paper bag.

"Oh, hey," said Estelle. "How'd it go?"

"Swift is still hanging around the pier," said Cass. "I think he wants to stay close enough to shore to see me."

"Or so I can feed him Zee's muffins," I added.

"Nah, he's there to see me," said Cass firmly. "The water's back to normal after Cameron's spell messed everything up."

"And he's in jail," Estelle added. "Was the Reaper around?"

"Nope, but I'm guessing he's coming to see Rory later."

I shrugged. "Probably."

"You still want him, even after seeing that scary guy?" She raised an eyebrow.

"He wasn't that scary," I said, and she snorted. "Anyway, life's too short to nit-pick on other people's joy."

"That's not what I meant," Cass said. "I mean—whatever." She walked away, after dropping the paper bag on the counter.

"I guess she's not going to help us, then?" Estelle adjusted her grip on her stack of books and carried them behind the desk.

"Apparently not." She'd left her paper bag on the front desk, though, and when I picked up, I saw the logo for Zee's bakery.

Not only was she not fighting with me, she'd also given me a muffin? Huh.

Munching on the muffin, I picked up the last two books from the front desk and took them to the Reading Corner. As per usual, the academy students had left a pile of rubbish behind, but at least there weren't any posters for secret societies. There'd been a brief attempt at an Aspiring Reapers Society that had shut down even faster than the vampires' one had. I suspected Nick's mother might have had something to do with that.

While everyone knew about the theft, the Reaper's appearance had sparked a whole flurry of new exaggerated legends about what had really gone down on the beach, carried in whispers between the students. For the last two days, Aunt Candace had been hidden in her writing cave. Rumour had it she was fictionalising hers and Dominic's doomed love story and that it was going to be her most epic tale yet. I hoped for all our sakes she'd leave the Reaper out of it.

I still hadn't met the man himself. Xavier hadn't brought him up either, though if I carried on spending time with him, it definitely wasn't the last I'd seen of the master of death.

But why worry about it? Whatever happened, we'd take it one day at a time.

The door creaked open, and I got to my feet, dusting myself off. Xavier was here, which meant the end of my shift.

I had a date with a Reaper.

ABOUT THE AUTHOR

Elle Adams lives in the middle of England, where she spends most of her time reading an ever-growing mountain of books, planning her next adventure, or writing. Elle's books are humorous mysteries with a paranormal twist, packed with magical mayhem.

She also writes urban and contemporary fantasy novels as Emma L. Adams.

Find Elle on Facebook at https://www.facebook.com/pg/ElleAdamsAuthor/